COWBOY MINE

3B Ranch Series (Book One)

REBECCA LYNN

authorHOUSE®

AuthorHouse™
1663 Liberty Drive
Bloomington, IN 47403
www.authorhouse.com
Phone: 1 (800) 839-8640

Published by AuthorHouse 02/02/2017

ISBN: 978-1-5246-6986-7 (sc)
ISBN: 978-1-5246-6985-0 (e)

CHAPTER ONE

**** Beau Blanton, Professional (PBR) Cup Rider donned the protective vest as he dialed the cell phone and counted the number of rings. He had about half an hour for his turn in the arena on one of the massive, perpetually angry bulls. As with many rodeo professionals there was a ritual that he and his family carried out and no way was he going to miss it. The last few minutes before a ride he spoke with his half sisters, Ava, who was ten, Kassandra, twelve and Geniveve, seventeen.

Failure to speak with them prior to his rides frequently spelled disaster in the arena. While he had faith in his strength and skill, for some reason he felt he needed all the help he could get today. He didn't have a good feeling today, but wasn't sure if it concerned his ride or something else. Since his mother's fiasco of a marriage to Rodney Smithe eighteen years ago and the many subsequent problems the man had created for the family and ranch, Beau's faith in the Almighty had been shaken. Beau ran his fingers through his hair and slapped his hat against his leg.

'Why did He allow that freakin' jerk to cause so much damage? Why did He allow a beautiful, innocent little baby to be born with the birth defects that she so bravely lived with? Why did my normally intelligent mother fall for such a selfish, egotistical fraud?'

This was the last event of the National Championships Cup Tour and he knew his mother and the girls would be waiting in front of the TV, listening for his call.

Finally, "Hello,....Dad?" A small, excited voice whispered breathlesly.

— 1 —

He breathed a sigh of relief and smiled at hearing the wonderful little voice. He loved being called daddy and felt more of a father than a brother. By calling him daddy, he knew Ava was alone in the large living room.

"Howdy, kiddo. How's my favorite lucky charm doin'?!" he said into his blue tooth.

"I knew it'd be you! We've been waiting! What took you so long? We almost missed it!" Ava squealed.

She had been born with Spina bifida, a devastating condition characterized by a hole in the spine. Unfortunately, her father, Rodney, had been furious and refused to accept that any child of his could be imperfect. He decided Lillie, his wife, had been unfaithful, had born the child of another man and then had tried to pass it off as his. He had from that day, wanted nothing to do with his wife or their youngest daughter.

Beau, on the other hand had taken one look at the beautiful little girl and was completely smitten. When she looked up at him and wrapped her tiny fist around his finger she had stolen his heart.

Disgusted with his step-father, and disappointed with his mother, Beau immedialy took charge of the baby's care and became both brother and father. He hired a full time nurse to ensure Ava's medical issues were seen to. He, his brother, Brett Jr. and their sister Bobbi had taken turns changing diapers, giving baths, and being chief cooks and bottle washers. They had all become adept at providing physical therapy and dispensing the prescribed medication as needed when the nurse was off.

As it turned out, their schedules had worked out so that one of them was always at home. Beau had become her legal guardian and would have willingly adopted her but his mother, Lillie, had refused to relinquish her parental rights. She was heartbroken that, 'Rodney the runt,' as Bobbi had dubbed him had turned his back on her because of their baby's physical problems. But instead of placing the responsibility for her husband's neglect and abandonment on his vanity and ego, she also had turned her back on the innocent child and still had little to do with her.

"So are you goin' to answer my question?" he asked with a chuckle.

Ava giggled. "I'm ok. Genny, and Kassi are helping Lillie with supper! They're makin' popcorn balls and we've got rootbeer floats! That way we can have snacks when we watch you ride! You are going to win right?!"

Beau smiled and felt warm all over. He loved all four of his younger sisters, but there was a special bond with Ava. "I'll do my best, honey. I drew, Good Ole Boy for the third ride, he's a 90 point bull, so we'll just have to see."

('Good Ole Boy' was widely known as one of the strongest, meanest bulls in the PBR Cup Circuit. More than once he had been called the next, 'Bodacious'. One of the most feared and respected bulls in rodeo history, but Beau took care to keep that fact from Ava). "I take it Bobbi isn't there?"

"No," Ava said, "She said she has a big, important case that she has been working on. She had to be in court for it today. A man was very mean to his niece, he hurt her and Bobbi said she's gonna, "Make him pay," mimicking their sister's voice.

Bobbi was the youngest child of his birth parents, Brett and Lillie Blanton. Now twenty-eight, she had been only five when their father had been killed in the arena by the bull he had drawn. She had few memories of him, but had flatly refused to accept Rodney in a paternal role much to Lillie's dismay. She had a deep hatred of her step father though she had never expressed why. She was now an attorney in the state of Montana, specializing in child welfare and family law.

Beau and Brett loved her, but they seldom saw eye to eye with her on anything with the exception of issues pertaining to their younger sister's welfare. She was confusing to her older brothers. She prefered suits, high heels and brief cases to Beau's jeans, boots and saddles or Brett's cammos, lace up boots and M-16s. Sometimes, she seemed totally content and happy in jeans and boots on the ranch then, she couldn't wait to be away from it.

"When you win, can you and Rowdy come home soon and bring the buckle?! I want to see it but I miss you and I worry about you. Will you do me a favor if I say pretty please and give you any extra big hug every day when you get home?"

He chuckled, "An extra big hug every day? That sounds like a mighty big favor?"

"It is....cause I know you won't want to do it."

"Well, tell me what this favor is that means so much to you, Tadpole."

Ava took a deep breath for courage. "I want you to wear the helmet. Would you please do that for me? Please?"

Beau sighed. "Aw babydoll, you know how much I hate those things."

"I know, daddy, but see....me and Kassi was watching a dvd about rodeos back in the olden days."

Beau chuckled. "Back in the olden days huh?"

"Yeah. They were back in the nineteen-nineties! Anyway," she became serious again. "There was this one bull, his name was Bodacious. He was this big, mean bull that jumped and bucked different from the others. He hurt a lot of cowboys, and there was this one cowboy, oooh Kassi and Gen said he was really hot. His name was Buck....Buck....oh I can't remember his last name."

"Hedeman, baby. Buck Hedeman."

"That's him! Anyway, there was this one bull. His name was Bodacious and he hurt this guy really bad. Bodacious bucked and hit him in face, and he flew up into the air and then went down on the ground and....and it was really bad....He looks really good now, but he had to have lots of operations and....I just don't want you to get hurt like that. Please." she begged.

CHAPTER TWO

**** Four pairs of eyes were glued to the flat screen tv. "Get off! Get off!" Genny jumped up and screamed at the tv.

"Jump! Beau, jump! Mom, his hand's caught in the rope!" Kassi yelled.

"Beau!" his mother said between gritted teeth. "Oh please let this be the last time! I can't do this any more."

Ava watched, horrified as her big brother tried in vain to get off and away from the furious bull. Her little fists were held tightly to her mouth as she began to softly sing, "My Sweet Matador" to her hero.

With the crowd roaring and clapping, Beau could have sworn he heard, "My Sweet Matador," on the wind. He saw Rowdy, the third bull fighter run in close and grasped his wrist as together they moved with the bull's frantic fight to be rid of them. Just as Rowdy freed his hand Beau flew through the air away from the bull, but not with the greatest of ease.

He landed hard, even with Rowdy's help and the soft dirt. He lay stunned for a moment while getting his breath back. "I give my love once more to My Sweet Ma-a-ta-door," floated around him.

'Damn, I must be delusional.' He thought. As he tried to take a deep breath. Unfortunately he had hit the ground hard enough to knock the breath right out of him.

"Dirt gets harder every year." he gasped and saw his best friend, Rowdy, rushing toward him and seeing the shape he was in motioned for help.

"That was a hell of a ride, Beau." Rowdy grinned. "No way is anybody beatin' that score. Anythin' broken?"

"Physically....I think maybe a rib or two, not sure about the leg. Mentally, I'm not so sure. I think I'm beginning to hallucinate from one too many head shots."

———⟡———

Beau, and Rowdy sat next to the 3B horse trailer, rootbeers in hand. Beau groaned softly as he adjusted in his seat. The bull had slammed him against the railing twice, ripping tendons and muscles, as well as bruising ribs and leaving one cracked. But he smiled smugly to himself, as he recalled how his step-father had laughed and jeered at his dream of being the Bull Riding National Champion.

"Not bad for the worthless no account Rodney the Runt always called me. Huh, Rowdy?" Following the last ride, the friends carried out another tradition by saluting his father's memory. Although tonight, because of Beau's prescribed pain medication the toast was with Dad's rootbeer instead of their usual Light beer. Beau closed his eyes, repositioned his leg on the wooden crate and breathed away the pain.

Rowdy chuckled. "Man, I can just see your pop up there whooping it up right now. Dad said they always dreamed of making it this far together like us, but to have you make that dream a reality for him would make him a very happy man. Brett would be here celebrating with us too if he weren't on deployment."

Master Chief Brett A. Blanton Jr, was somewhere over seas on assignment, or he would have been standing in the crowd tonight, and Beau had no doubt that his brother's voice would have been loudest of all. Brett, Brody, and Rowdy had always been his biggest fans, and best friends.

Beau grinned, "Brody would have been cheerin' ya on as well, and you know that your sister was watchin'." He looked at Rowdy who just pretended his twin's name wasn't mentioned.

Rowdy studied his friend closely, "Trish?! Ha! She hates me. She has for years. Ever since...." he shook his head and changed the subjct, "How ya feelin', bro?" He could tell that Beau would crash soon. He was on some high grade pain meds and was nearly nodding off. The new champ looked like crap and most likely felt like it as well.

Beau fought down another yawn. After his winning ride, he had spent an hour in the ER. He would wear a leg brace for six - eight weeks and had been ordered to use crutches to get around. His right arm was also wrapped and sore. Following his release from the ER he had returned to the rodeo and spent a good four hours having his picture taken, giving interviews, and signing autographs. He loved the life, but had to admit that sometimes the screaming teenage girls and wanta be teenage tuff guys were a bit much. But he loved and looked forward to the children. Their bright eyed innocence and shy admiration made the time worthwhile.

He loved the exuberance of the little boys and the bashful glances of the little girls as they offered a rodeo program or picture to be signed. He didn't even mind the creaky knees as he normally squatted and pulled them close for a picture. The memory of pink cheeks, shining eyes and shy smiles as the precious signature was caught close to their little chests when they shrugged and murmured their thanks got him through many difficult moments.

"I'm doing as well as can be expected." The new champ answered tiredly. Beau caught a glimpse of his reflection in the silver tin siding of the trailer. Even to his own eyes he looked exhausted. He studied his appearance, and just could not see why so many young girls and women were dead set on winning his hand. He was nothing special.

He was a man used to manual labor, and it showed. Beau was a big man; all muscle from the years of working on the family ranch, then the Rangers, and all the years as a rodeo cowboy. He was six foot one, with broad shoulders, deep chest and washboard abs. He had short dark hair, that he preferred to be keep in a near military style and cobalt blue eyes, that shown with an intelligence that shocked most fans.

With an IQ of one hundred and forty-six, he could have been a doctor or a lawyer. A fact that his mother started reminding him of after marrying his step-father, Rodney. Beau often reminded her that he was a weapons expert, as well as a trained martial artist and had a degree in business management from an accredited online school. However, none of that meant anything to his mother anymore. He had followed in his father's footsteps, and understood his mother's fear. Brett Blanton Sr. had been one of the greatest rodeo cowboys in the country. Until one fateful day when he was unseated by a bull named, 'Widow Maker'.

That day the huge black and white bull proved just how he'd gotten that name. Brett Sr's untimely death (a death that some still claimed was no ordinary bull riding accident) had been only six months after Beau's tenth birthday.

This had been a long stretch away from the ranch. He and Rowdy hadn't been home in four months. For him, each season had become more difficult. He worried about Ava and their mother's continuing negativity toward her. He felt the need to be in his own house on the ranch full time so he could move the little girl in with him thereby providing a more positive atmosphere. He was tired of his mother's nagging to leave the rodeo and take over his responsibilities at the ranch.

His cell phone began vibrating and jiggling on the crate. He groaned and Rowdy rolled his eyes upon recognizing Lillie's picture as the caller ID. He reached down, put it on speaker and answered in the same way he had for years, with a sigh of resignation and, "Blanton."

"Beau....," she sounded as if she'd been crying. Both men sat up straighter, now fully alert and locked gazes. They immediately had the same thought. Both men leaned forward to hear.

"....Beau,...." she fought back a sob as she tried to speak.

"Mom, calm down. Take a breath and tell me what's happened." That feeling that something was amiss returned and he felt a chill.

"Beau, I need....it's....it's...." she couldn't continue and broke into heartrending sobs.

Yancy, the ranch foreman took the phone, "Beau, is Rowdy there, son?"

Rowdy sat up straight, "I'm here, Pa. What's up?"

"We....got a situation here guys."

Emerald green eyes met cobalt blue as the life long friends looked at each other and said, "Are the girls ok?"

"The girls are fine, all proud as punch of both of ya. No, Lillie received a letter from Brett's Commanding Officer today." He sighed and took a deep breath. "Brett has been listed as Missing in Action. Lillie and the girls would sure appreciate you guys bein' home right now.

Beau closed his eyes tight, let out a hard breath and tried to wet his suddenly dry lips. When he was finally able to speak his voice was low and gravely. "How?" Was all he could force out.

"Two weeks ago....they were comin' back from a mission. The helicopter was struck by a missile of some kind. It went down in a remote area, no survivers found so far. Several are unaccounted for. He and his swim buddy Nico are two of 'em. That's all we know."

Both men closed their eyes. Rowdy leaned forward and squeezed his friend's shoulder. He cleared his throat, "Thanks, pop. Um, we need to take care of some loose ends here and then we'll start for home. It'll take us a few days, but I think we should be able to make it there by Saturday." He was horrified to find his own voice cracking.

Beau wiped his hand down his face, and took a deep breath to steady himself. "Are mom and the girls ok? Does Bobbie know?"

Having regained some composure Lillie answered, "We're all all right son. The girls are in shock and Ava keeps asking for you. Yancy is here with us. We can't get hold of Barbara till this evening after court. I....don't know what I would have done without Yancy. You....you boys drive safely back now ok? Promise me. Beau....son....I want you to know how proud I am of you. How proud I've always been, even when I was silly enough to not voice it."

Beau assured her they would and thanked Yancy, the father figure for whom he had so much respect, admiration and affection. Yancy had stepped in and was there for the family following Brett Sr's death. Despite having lost his best friend he was a tower of strength.

A tall man with dark brown, slightly greying hair, and laughing green eyes (just like his son's), Yancy had been a role model for Beau and Brett especially after their father died. They managed the ranch together and Yancy had been in charge during Brett Sr's time on the road with the rodeo.

It killed Beau to know that little Ava kept asking for him, but knew that Yancy would look after her and the rest of his girls until he could get there.

"Tell Ava and the girls that we'll be back as soon as we can." he replied.

"I will. The church is planning a prayer service in place of the regular service Sunday. We....we watched your ride, Beau....Brett would be so proud of you both tonight, and so am I,"....She took a shakey breath," Bye, boys. See you in a few days." With that she hung up the phone.

Rowdy pressed the end button, turned off the speaker and handed the phone to his friend. When Beau did not accept the device, Rowdy slipped it into the cowboy's front shirt pocket. Beau just sat there, staring into space shaking his head. Realizing his friend was in shock and unable to believe the news Rowdy slapped his knees and stood.

"Well, I'll start gettin' things together and grab us some grub from the venders. We can eat on the way as we're hungry."

Beau shook his head to clear it. "Uh, yeah, yeah, that's good. I'll get some ice and restock the cooler and get things travel ready in the trailer."

"Bro, you go get some shut eye while you can, leave everything else to me." Rowdy crossed his arms and gave his best friend a pointed look.

Beau nodded, "Thanks, bro." And headed for bed.

CHAPTER THREE

Four months later-

**** Drina Skylard and her band, "The Skydivers," sat back stage relaxing and celebrating after the last concert of the tour. Drina was small, one hundred and twenty-five pounds soaking wet and barely five feet three, with long, curly blonde hair, and glacier blue eyes. When she smiled she lit up the room. Sleeping on a foldout couch across the room lay her ten year old half-brother Kyle, his twin sister Kaylee and Eli, the eleven year old son of her best friend and Fiddler, Riley.

Drina's mother and step-father had died in a plane crash three years earlier. She had taken legal guardianship for her younger siblings, and would walk through fire for them. She knew however that this was no life for the twins. They loved traveling with her, but it came with a price. They had no friends save for the Band members, the crew and Eli. All three were beginning to talk about riding a bus, being on baseball and basket ball teams. Even the much more studious Kaylee was beginning to complain about having the same tutor year after year and the lack of girlfriends. So Drina had decided to take the twins on a long vacation and Eli too, if Riley would allow it.

Drina sat back, exhausted and closed her eyes. "I think I need to turn in, guys, I feel like a limp rag." she said, never opening her eyes.

Her drummer Brón McMillan, turned to look at her. "I thought ya said ye had a surprise for the rug rats?" he asked in his deep Scottish bur. When on stage the drummer spoke very properly, but once he was out of the limelight he fell right back into his own way of speaking. When the band had first met him he had been the brunt of a lot of jokes, now it was just an every day thing everyone took for granted.

His girlfriend Amy McDonald nodded her head, red curls bouncing. "Aya, lass. Ye did say that." Drina was always amazed at how the little Irish clogger could have such a musical voice.

"Yes! That's right, thanks for the reminder." She nodded and lowered her voice to a whisper. "Anyway, I decided we need a vacation." She looked at her siblings fondly. "Those two have been through so much what with losing their folks, leaving their home, school and friends and being on the road with us all the time....the three of us need a vacation. So I did some research online and found a working Dude Ranch in Montana called the 3B Ranch run by Beau Blanton."

Ben Ford, her lead guitarist and one of her two BFF's breathed, "The Bull Riding National Champion?! Eli and I saw his winning ride! Man, that guy can ride! He's said to be this century's bull riding prodigy. Riley, Eli and I have all been following his career since he got out of the Army Rangers. I guess he excelled there too. From what I understand he's highly decorated. A true war hero. The guy just doesn't stop. Eli always yells along with the croud as he says his lucky catchphrase. He does it after he mounts up, every time. It's kind of traditional for him and his fans."

His wife, Riley, (Drina's BFF since childhood and the band's fiddler), grinned and sat in his lap. "Let's getty up and go!" She giggled, "He's right, Drina, Blanton is without a doubt the best, this year he even out rode Adrienne M. That man is incredible! Unfortunately, he announced last night that Good Ole Boy was his last ride. He's retiring undefeated. He said he intends to run his ranch and help raise his little sisters. I heard his older brother went MIA a few months ago." she wrapped an arm around her husband's neck, sadness in her eyes. "I can't even imagine what that must be like."

Amy sighed, "Poor boyô. He has so much on his shoulders."

Drina nodded. "Yes, I've heard a lot about his military history also. He saved the lives of over twenty soldiers, at the risk of his own life. He even risked his life to retrieve the bodies of his fallen comrades. I can't imagine what kind of courage he must have. I did some research on the Army Rangers after I learned he was one. I was amazed at what I found. The Creed itself is scary. You have to really truly want to be a Ranger to go through with that. Not to mention how utterly hot he is in both chaps or uniform."

She cleared her thoat at the looks her friends gave her. "Anyway, as I was saying, I've already booked a three bedroom cabin for three months. I'm going on hiatus for a while. I've already talked with Jerry, he'll make sure you all keep getting your checks so don't worry about that. I'm burnt out, I'm tired and need some time to really connect with the kids. They need to be kids again. The plan is....to relax, have some fun, and get my flame back. And who knows....I may become inspired while we're there."

Both Riley and Ben looked at each other. She could ride a horse with the best of them, but pleasure riding, and driving cattle were two very different things. They were both thinking the same thing. Their little Drina was tough as nails, and had a temper to boot. But the twins were having increasingly more problems.

Kyle was all boy. A cute little trouble maker that was always finding himself in some kind of situation, and those were becoming more frequent and problematic. Kaylee was more than a little shy and preferred to curl up in a chair with a book. But, she had retreated even more since their parents death.

All three of the kids loved the rodeo and were huge fans of Beau Blanton, and Rowdy Kincaid. They would jump through the roof when they learned it was his ranch they were going to stay at. The hands at the 3B weren't going to know what hit them, nor would Mr. Beau Blanton.

Riley smiled, "Have you put in any thought as to how you're going to get Odin there?" Ben nodded his agreement with his new wife.

Drina sighed, "Not really." she whispered back. "I just haven't had a chance to stop and think about it, but I'm open to suggestions. I very highly doubt the airport would let me take a horse into First Class."

Ben chuckled, "No. I don't think they would."

Riley grinned conspiratorially, "I might have an idea, I don't know if you would like it, though."

Drina opened her eyes and looked at her Best friends. "At this point I'm willing to listen to anything, besides you always have good ideas."

Grayson Daniels (who played the keyboard for the group) chuckled. "She does at that." Gray said.

Riley tossed a pillow at her older brother and sniped back. "I don't hear you coming up with any suggestions, Gracie!"

The smile left his face as he turned on his younger sister. "Don't call me Grrr-acie! Geez! I was just teasin', Riley!" He snarled between gritted teeth.

Ben stood and put Riley in the chair and held a hand up for silence. "Just stop. This is the very reason a vacation is a good idea. We're all tired, we're all burnt out. We've been together nearly 24/7 for a long time and we've had a lot going on. We all need this break. What we don't need is to be at each other's throats."

He turned to his bride of eleven months and raised his eyebrow and motioned toward his brother-in-law.

Riley sighed. "I'm sorry, Gray. I shouldn't have jumped you like that. I know you didn't mean anything. Still friends?" she asked pleadingly.

"No prob. I jumped too quickly too. Man! We are all soooo tired."

Ben looked at his wife and smiled, "Now, what was your idea, baby?"

She shot her brother an apologetic look before saying, "I was just thinking that we could use the trailer and transport Odin and our horses there ourselves. We could," she smiled and raised her eyebrows, "maybe take it slow and stop at campsites between here and Montana and use it as a honeymoon." She looked at each person in turn. "What do ya think?"

Drina smiled and sat up. "That is actually not a bad idea. Now that I think of it I think I remember seeing that the ranch has a honeymoon cabin off to itself. It would be perfect for you two and Eli could bunk with Kyle in his room. I can get an extra ticket and take him with me so you two can have all the time to yourselves. In fact I'll double check and book the cabin in the morning."

The Scotsman chuckled, "Might I remind ya, lad....that ye have a three horse trailer, and all together ye have to transport four critters."

Ben looked at his best friend with a frown. He hated being called lad, and the drummer knew it. "I take it you have an idea?"

Brón nodded. "You can use me own trailer. It be a four horse rig, with a tackroom, and full camper built in."

Four weeks later....

Ben and Riley met Drina, Kaylee and the two boys at the airport. Riley hugged her son and the other kids and they all tried talking at once. They moved toward the baggage claim while Ben left to pick up the SUV that Drina had reserved.

"How long's it gonna take to get there?" Eli asked his mom as they swung hands through the airport. "Well, we're going to have a picnic lunch at a rest stop about a half hour from here. That will give us all a chance to eat, stretch our legs and get the horses out for some exercise."

"Did you bring my pony?" Eli asked his mother hopefully.

"Yes, we brought Watson, Ginger, Odin, and Thunder."

An hour later found the group finally on their way with Drina and the three kids leading the small caravan. Kaylee was in front and as usual, had her nose in a book. The boys were in the back seat getting bored and rambunctious.

"Are we there yet?" Kyle asked. "We're gettin' tired of riding, at least in a car."

"Not there yet, we've got maybe....an hour, hour and a half to go." Drina answered, "We're getting close though."

"Close? How can you say we're gettin' close if there's still an hour and a half to go?" Eli asked.

"Because the farms and ranches out here live well away from towns and cities. It isn't unusual for them to have to drive an hour to get to the closest town. That's why some of the more prosperous ranchers or farm settlements have a small plane or helicopter in case of emergencies."

"Gee, I didn't know you were takin' us totally out a civilization." Kyle mumbled.

Kaylee rolled her eyes and shook her head, "He's such a boy."

One hour later-

Drina had just ordered the boys to stop tossing pillows at each other when Eli asked, "Are we there ye-e-et? Holy Moly! What the he....uh, heck is that?"

"That my young friend is called a gate." Drina answered trying to hide her smile.

"Why do they have a gate? What's the fence for?" Kyle demanded. He and Eli looked at each other with some trepidation. "Uh, Drina? We don't mean nuthin' when we get in trouble ya know. I mean if this is one of those tough love, marine kind of places, we really don't mean nuthin'."

She looked in the rear view mirror and worked hard to keep a straight face. She glanced at Kaylee to see if she had the same misunderstanding. She was surprised to see her sister's book fall to the floor while her nose was flattened to the window and she was staring open mouthed through the fence.

"Kaylee, what are you looking at, hon?" When the child turned to look at Drina her eyes were huge and there was a smile on her face that had been absent for too long. "What is it, honey?"

The girl was jumping in her seat with excitement. "There are some cowboys out there. Real, truly live cowboys with hats and spurs and chaps and....everything! They're riding horses like....fast!" She lowered her voice to a whisper, "And they're gorgeous!"

She giggled, shrugged and turned back to the window and put it down. She smiled and waved to the cowboys as they rode even with the suv. One looked at her and smiled, winked, took his hat off and waved it in the air at her showing his deep copper hair. Kaylee clasped her hands over her heart, grinned shyly, shrugged and waved back with a huge grin.

Beau Blanton looked at Rowdy Kincaid and grinned. "I don't know what it is about you that ensnares all those feminine hearts."

Rowdy grinned and sighed, "You either got it....or ya don't."

CHAPTER FOUR

**** Beau pulled Kitt, (his large white stallion) up short and watched as none other than Drina Skylard step out of the large SUV.

Rowdy's pocket buzzed and he pulled out his cell phone, looked at the screen and grimaced. "Well, bro....Ava is askin' for my help at the arena."

Beau nodded and watched his best friend lope off. He turned back and watched Miss Skylard unload her bags, as three of the cutest kids Beau had ever seen followed her out of the van. All three looked to be nine or ten years old. The boys jumped out and immediately began looking around, huge smiles on their faces. The girl, slid out of the truck with an enthusiasm that was much more controlled. She looked excited, yet more than a bit nervous and was all eyes; big, dark eyes. A look of comprehension accompanied a small smile.

She pulled on Drina's arm, "That's one of the cowboys that rode beside us." she whispered, as she indicated the cowboy in the far distance.

Beau watched a big silver Chevy Silverado pull up behind them hauling an impressive four horse trailer.

"Not a bad lookin' rig." he admired aloud to himself.

As the boss, Beau preferred to meet and greet the new guests himself when possible. He felt it was up to him and/or Rowdy to get a feel of the personalities as they came, and to help get them settled into their rooms for the night. The ranch offered riding lessons for beginners which were usually run by his sister Genny, and the new hire David. In special cases however, Beau or Rowdy stepped in personally. They liked to see for themselves how everyone, particularly kids reacted around the horses.

Kaylee grabbed her big sister's hand with a loud gasp of shock. She had just realized who the cowboy galloping their way was. Drina looked down and noticed that Kaylee, Kyle and Eli were all staring down the long drive. She looked up and saw the biggest, toughest, sexiest man she had ever seen cantering their way. Her jaw nearly dropped when it hit her just who the man was. She knew he was a part owner of the 3B, but it had never once occured to her that he would actually take part in it.

Beau pulled Kitt to a stop and tipped his hat. "Howdy, folks." he drawled while dismounting. "Welcome to the 3B, where y'all come in as Greenhorns and leave as genu-ine Cowpokes. My name is...."

He never had a chance to finish when Eli and the twins all squeaked out his name, huge grins on their faces. "Beau Blanton!" they cried excitedly.

Beau gave them all a smile and shook their hands formally. "And who might you be?" He asked.

Kyle stepped forward, hooked his thumbs through his belt loops, a mirror image of Beau's stance. "My name is Kyle, this is my sister Kaylee....we're twins, and this is my best friend Eli." He pointed to the big truck, "That's Riley, she's Eli's mom and Ben, he's Eli's step dad. They're newly weds so they spend a lot o' time doing kissy face and huggin' an' holdin' hands." He turned slightly and thumbed toward his other sister, "This is Drina, she's older than us an she's our half sister, but we don't pay no attention to the half part. She's our guardian too, since our mom and dad died in a plane crash. Our dad wasn't really her dad. She had a different one," (thumbing again toward Drina) "but we all had the same mom. She was married to both our dads, but not at the same time. Drina's sort of like a mom now 'ceptin she'd have to adopt us to be that, an we all like the guardian thing cause that way we all still only have one mom an' we don't think we could get used to callin' her mom any hows. Drina's famous like you only she don't ride bulls, jus' horses. She sings and plays a bunch of instruments like the guitar, violin, and piano. She makes lots of recordings and personal appearances." Kyle took a huge breath and nodded his head once.

Beau, worked hard to still a chuckle of pure joy and nodded, "I see. That's all good to know. I hope y'all are goin' to have a great time here."

Drina was dumbstruck by the ease in which their host had the boys talking and laughing. She had especially begun to worry about Kaylee's unusual reticence of late. 'Maybe this really will be good for all of us', she thought to herself as she admired the cowboy before them.

She had thought at first that he was a bit of a stuff shirt due to the way he deliberately avoided her eyes. She wasn't used to being ignored by the male population. She had hoped this would be a time of non celebrity....now that she had experienced it, she wasn't sure she liked it.

"Well," Beau stated as he slapped his work gloves against his leg. "What say we get your horses settled. I bet they're mighty tired of bein' stuffed in that trailer. What's they're names?" He asked, finally meeting Drina's gaze. "Are any of them goin' to require any special quarters?"

Drina frowned. "No, none of them will require anything special, other than that one stall needs to be good sized because my horse stands sixteen hands. The mare and geldings are standards and a pony."

"The pony is mine," Eli announced. "His name is Watson."

"Ah, elementary Watson. Don't think we've ever had a Watson before. Had a basset hound called Sherlock once. We also have former-Army Ranger, Marines, and SEALs that works on the ranch. One in particular, is a Ranger, he's in charge of ranch security. His call sign in the Rangers was Sherlock. He still answers to it from time to time."

Eli's face lit up and he grinned, wholly enjoying himself. "Mom, did ya hear that? He likes Sherlock Holmes too!"

"I heard, baby," His mother said putting her arm around his thin shoulders and pulled him close for a hug.

Eli's face flamed red. "Oh, mo-om, don't call me baby now! Geeze!" and pulled away from her.

"It's ok, Eli," Ben spoke softly to his step son, "Maybe while we're here, she'll figure out you're not a baby any more."

"It hope so." he mumbled.

"Don't let it rile ya none, son." Beau said, "My mom slips up now and then and still calls me baby." He rolled his eyes. "The rest of us just pretend we don't hear anything." He spoke to the adults then, "Half our stalls are oversized. Do ya need help gettin' 'em out?" he asked, walking over and looking through one of the windows. He whistled, "Those are some mighty fine horses."

"Thanks," Drina and Riley said together.

"So....Watson is Eli's, who do the others go with?" He asked admiring them all.

Drina walked over to the trailer, "The mare, Ginger, is Riley's, Thunder, the gelding is Ben's and....

"The stallion is yours?" Beau asked incredulously. He looked Drina up and down and pushed his hat up with one finger. "Little thing like you rides that much horse?" he asked working hard to hide his smile.

A few days ago Lillie had informed him of the country star's reservations so he had done some research on her. He found he liked most of her music, but was unimpressed by her choice in attire. It was too flashy. If she planned on wearing that kind of clothing here she wouldn't last five minutes working with the cattle and horses, they'd stampede from the flash. Having met her in person however, he might have to revise his opinion of her. She obviously had a temper and could look after herself. She was definitely a little firecracker and much too pretty for his piece of mind.

'Whew!' He thought to himself, 'This lady was way too sexy to herd cattle.' But he couldn't wait to see her on that horse.

Drina took a deep breath, silently counted to ten and crossed her arms and frowned. "Thanks for the offer and concern," she said icily, "We usually take care of our own horses but no, I don't need any help, I can handle him and all the others if I need to," then added sarcastically, "I'm sure I can manage. If you have to give that much help around women you must know some pretty sissified girls."

"Well, ma'am. This is a dude ranch, and a lot of sissified people do come here, but they leave un-sissified." Beau answered.

Riley turned away from her friend to hide a chuckle. The three kids stared at the songbird.

"Geez! Drina." Kyle said embarrassed, "You just insulted some of the people that come here! If we'd done that you'd have grounded us."

"Drina! That was so rude. I can't believe you did that. You insulted Mr. Blanton too. He might not let us stay now, and....and I was beginning to think that maybe I could be able to, you know, learn to not be afraid to ride." Kaylee said shyly, huge tears welling up in her big brown eyes.

Drina looked down and took a deep breath. "They're right, Mr. Blanton. This is one of the reasons why we're here. We've been on the road for eleven months, we're tired and too touchy." She looked him in the eye, "I'm not trying to excuse my behaviors; the kids are right. I shouldn't have talked to you like that. I'm sorry."

Beau smiled, tipped his hat and said, "Apology accepted, ma'am. Most folks come here to regroup and get acquainted to who they used to be, or who they want to be." He pointed to his men who had just ridden up. "We all want to help. That's what this ranch is all about. These are some of my men that you'll all be seein' a lot of." He pointed to each in turn, "This is Yancy, he's my forman, this here is Topper, Tad, he's new, and that there's Nathan or...." he grinned at Eli. "Sherlock. He's our security expert. That there is David, he's also a new hire." As he introduced, each man in turn smiled and tipped his hat.

Yancy stepped forward, "We like ta come down the road, and it's a lot o' fun for us to give kids a ride back to the outfit. It let's us get to know each other."

The boys whooped and, "All right!" Kyle grinned.

"Yeees!" Eli shouted.

Kaylee looked panic stricken yet hopeful as she looked at the horses.

Beau walked over and squatted before her so they were at near eye level. "Now, I couldn't help but hear that you might be a little fearful about bein' around or on horses?" He asked gently.

She nodded shyly, "I want to ride, but....I....I got trampled." huge tears rolled down her cheeks. "I know I'm being a baby."

"Whoa down there. It is not being a baby to fear something that out weighs ya by a thousand pounds. It sounds to me like you have good reason to fear horses."

Yancy stepped forward and knelt down beside his friend and boss. "Not only is there nothing wrong with bein' afraid, but it takes a lot of courage to admit it."

Kaylee looked up hopefully, "Courage? Really?"

"Courage....Yes, ma'am." Beau assured and winked. "I'd be real pleased if you'd allow me an' Kitt to take ya up to the ranch, lil' Missy."

She looked at the huge white horse standing by nibbling at some roadside grass. She took a fearful step away from the huge cuttin' horse and looked down.

"Kitt's a real nice horse, I trained him myself. He's used to bein' around any kind of person or animal there is. He rides real smooth and easy and doesn't scare or buck. He won't do anything I don't tell him to do....please?" and held out his hand.

Kaylee looked up at Drina and Riley, "Could I, Drina?"

"If you want to," she smiled, "go ahead, have fun and we'll meet you up there."

Kaylee took Beau's hand and walked beside him. Once beside the horse, Beau gently grasped the bridle and pulled Kitt's head around. "Kitt, this is Kaylee and she's gonna let us take her back to the ranch." The horse whiffed Kaylee's neck and she giggled and leaned into Beau's side. "Is that all right, Kitt?"

The horse nodded several times and whuffed her dark hair before pointing his nose toward the saddle, as if to say, 'It's fine by me. Let's go!'

"You're goin' to stay at a nice, slow, smooth pace for her aren't ya, Kitt?"

Beau smiled when Kitt shook his head, as if to say. 'No!'

"Kitt, this little lady is a little frightened. We need to show her how much fun it is to ride and have a friend. Will you go slow for her?"

Kitt looked at Beau, then at Kaylee, then nodded his head in agreement, and the cowboy turned to look at Kaylee who was grinning from ear to ear.

"Ready?" Beau asked as the boys climbed up on the other horses behind the ranch hands.

"Ready." she said, smiling.

He put a foot in the stirrup and sprang into the saddle with out the use of his hands. She gasped at the show of strength and horsemanship. He reached down, picked her up easily and placed her in front of him in the saddle and said, "Ok, Miss Kaylee, tell him to go."

She grinned and reached out to pat the shiny white neck, clicked her tongue and said, "Giddy up, Kitt."

CHAPTER FIVE

**** Beau let out a long whistle, looked down into the brown eyes and smiled at Kaylee. "Is she always this touchy?" he whispered conspiratorially to her.

Drina called out from the drivers seat of the SUV, "I am not touchy!" she snapped.

Kaylee grinned, shrugged and nodded. She surprised him when she leaned back against his chest and whispered back. "Yeah, she is sometimes, but it's been a lot worse lately."

"Yeah?" He asked, "Sooo wh...."

The rest of their conversation was lost to Drina when he touched his heels to Kitt's sides and they rode ahead. She watched the two as she followed and was amazed at how often she saw Kaylee laugh and talk to look up and back at the cowboy. She smiled and settled back against the seat. 'This whole thing is worth it just to see the smile reach Kaylee's eyes and heart.' She looked up to the small picture of her mom and step-dad that was kept on the sun visor. *'Thanks for the dream idea guys, with your help and God's guidance, the three of us will be ok.'* She kissed her fingers and lovingly touched the picture.

Upon reaching the stables, she followed the asphalt lane and parked the SUV where two cowboys immediately began unloading the luggage and pointed out the cabin that would be her family's home for the next three months. She walked over to the barn lot where Ben was parking the horse trailer. Not far from the corral Beau was lifting Kaylee down from the saddle. Drina chuckled at the way her sister was steadily talking to both man and horse while gently petting Kitt's soft nose.

When the animal nuzzled her neck, Kaylee giggled and rewarded the white miracle with gentle strokes down the long neck.

Man and girl talked steadily as they walked over to stand beside her.

"Did you see me, Drina?" Kaylee was almost jumping up and down excitedly. "Once we started moving I wasn't scared. I didn't freeze up or panic. Now, I can pet him and stand right next to him and, and it.... feels really good. I think I'm ready to ride by myself."

She grabbed her older sister's hand and held it in both her own. "Thank you for bringing us here." Kaylee was ecstatic about her new courage and confidence and Drina was struck again by the feeling that they had indeed been led to the ranch.

"Yes I did. I'm proud of you, it's not easy facing a fear like that, but you did. I'm so glad you're having a good time already."

She looked over Kaylee's head and mouthed; 'Thank you,' to Beau.

He smiled and touched the brim of his hat in cowboy speak. "She did just fine. We'll make a cowgirl of her in no time. In fact," he rubbed his chin thoughtfully; "I think I know just the right geldin' for her. Totally trained, real calm, good bloodlines..." He nodded to himself, "Topper is beginnin' to use him with my youngest sister, Ava. He's good with her but she needs something a little bit smaller."

Kaylee's eyes widened, "Do you really think I could, Mr. Blanton?"

He smiled and ran the back of his fingers down her cheek. "It's Beau, lil' miss and yeah. I think he'll be perfect for you. We'll bring him out and see what he says. We let our horses guide us as to which rider is right. You'd be surprised how right they can be. For example....I didn't choose Kitt. He chose me."

"What's his name? When can I see him?"

"Hmm." He frowned. "Ya know, I'm not sure he has a name yet. If he doesn't and you two get along, that can be your first job. Comin' up with a name that fits."

As they were absorbed in their conversation, Ben and Riley had opened and gone inside the large trailer, and began the process of unloading the horses. Riley led her mare out and was followed by Ben with his gelding. They were met by another cowboy who led them to a fenced in area to stretch and enjoy some exercise after being locked up. Drina stepped in next and began talking to Odin.

"Hey, Odin, my big, beautiful boy," she crooned.

Beau raised his eyebrows, and looked at Kaylee, "Odin? As in one of the Norse gods?" He asked quietly.

"Yeah," Kaylee said, "Drina's into all that Thor, and Odin stuff."

"Really?" He leaned closer, "She doesn't have any of those Xena outfits does she?"

Kaylee slapped a hand over her mouth in a vain attempt to hide her giggles. Having just rejoined them, Ben and Riley tried to hide their amusement at the remark but lost themselves in laughter instead.

"I heard that." Came from inside as Drina stepped out onto the trailer ramp and glared at the four of them. Beau enjoyed watching Kaylee's eyes sparkle as she continued to giggle. He couldn't wait to get her and Ava together. He thought they would make a good match. Odin's head appeared and Beau stared as Drina led the beautiful blue roan stallion out and away from the trailer.

When he began to step toward the impressive animal Drina emperiously put her hand out. "Don't come any closer." She warned, "He doesn't tolerate men."

Beau simply smiled, nodded and slowly put his hand out toward the horse. Drina was about to order him back again when Odin stretched his neck and sniffed at the offered hand. Drina watched in amazement as Odin closed the distance and preceeded to snuff at Beau's hand and then nuzzled the man's neck. Beau grinned and chuckled as he gently caressed the animal's neck. "Oh yeah, you're a big mean boy aren't ya, fella?" He chuckled again as Odin whuffed at his hair and knocked off his black Stetson.

Kaylee giggled, "He likes to do that but mainly just to my sister, and Riley."

When Drina was about to admonish Odin for being unfaithful, Rowdy joined the group. "Sorry to interrupt, boss; but Ava sent me to fetch ya to the arena. Genny is gettin' frustrated. Ava says somethin's not right but they can't figure out what. Genny was turnin' the air blue when I left. I figured this is more a job for her Big Brother, not me."

He turned to the new comers, smiled and tipped his hat in typical cowboy greeting. "Sorry for the interruption, folks," he said. He peeked around Beau, waved, winked and grinned at Kaylee who was hiding behind him and turning pink. "Hey there," he said gently, "I'm...."

Kaylee stepped around the taller cowboy, grinned shyly, and breathed in a hushed, reverent tone, "Rowdy Kincaid."

Beau raised his eyebrows, shook his head and looked at his friend with a smile. "Another one bites the dust." he chuckled to himself.

Drina, who along with Ben and Riley looked on in amazement, smiled and said to Beau, "I take it this is a common occurrence here?" Drina couldn't help but notice that the newest cowboy's emerald green eyes were dull. As if he had, lost someone or something very dear to him, and had never fully healed from the pain of it.

"Yup. He draws 'em like a bee to honey. Girls seem to love both the scars and the tattoos."

Drina chewed on her lower lip and looked worriedly at her younger, impressionable sister.

Beau smiled, "Don't worry, he's as gentle with a young heart as he is with a yearlin' filly. They leave lovin' him and he remembers every one. Keeps in contact with a lot of 'em, kind of like a big brother. Last year he went to the High School Graduation of a young lady. She was one of our equine therapy patients." He turned to his friend, "Any idea what's goin' on?"

Rowdy shook Drina's hand, his grip was firm. She noticed that his left arm was covered in a tattoo sleeve. They all seemed to cover one huge mass of scars. Across his throat was a particularly nasty scar, that seemed to run across the voice box. 'That explains his husky voice.' She thought, and just under his right eye was a half moon scar that ran from the inner corner of his eye and down the length of his right cheek.

Rowdy rubbed his face and grimaced, "Weeell, I think it might have somethin' to do with the actual horse she's usin'. Ava told me a that Gen insisted on ridin' that young stud we've been workin' with. The rescue."

Beau pursed his lips, "The one we told her wasn't safe to be around yet; if ever?"

"Yyyyuup. That's the one. I believe he's the one the boys call Psyco." Rowdy said and winked at Kaylee. "Bet you never disobey rules do ya?"

"Yeah right!" Kyle scoffed jumping in on the conversation after he and Eli met the group. "Her? Disobey the rules? She thinks she has to be Miss Perfect."

"You should try it sometime, Kyle. I might have a peaceful night's sleep occasionally." Drina shot him a stern look that said to drop it and get off his twin's case.

"Well," Beau said and turned to Drina. "Let's go get Odin, and the others settled and get things straightened out with my younger siblings at the same time."

Always ready to jump in and help, Rowdy stepped toward Odin and reached for the lead shank only to have to rescue his knuckles from being bitten. He stepped back as Odin flattened his ears and bared his teeth.

Beau's lips twitched as he hid a smirk, "He doesn't tolerate men." he mimicked Drina smoothly, took the lead shank out of Drina's hands and turned toward the stables. Rowdy and Drina stood staring at the man and horse walking amicably beside each other.

"Wow!" Kyle exclaimed. "He never lets anyone walk him except Drina, and Riley. Even Ben can't touch him!" He looked at his older sister in awe.

"Well, I suppose there might be a few men that Odin will like. Don't know why he had to choose him though!" Drina kicked at the dirt and mumbled to herself grumpily.

Kyle grinned and started after the retreating figures.

Rowdy grinned and motioned for Drina to follow and gallantly held his elbow out to Kaylee. She grinned and shyly took his arm. "Don't let it bother you, ma'am. The man's never met a horse that didn't fall at his feet in the first two minutes." He said wryly, shaking his head. "Puts the rest of us to shame."

Rowdy and Beau gave the six a tour of the stables ending with Odin's stall. Drina had to admit that Odin settled in very well and left him contentedly munching on hay.

The group went to the closed in arena next door. Drina was impressed with the manner in which both men enteracted with the ranch hands, speaking to each one, asking about family members, answering questions, offering suggestions as needed.

"Do you know everybody that works here?" Kyle asked.

Beau chuckled, "Yep, pretty much. That's part of our job as the bosses. What kind of leaders would we be if we didn't know the people we're leadin'? A place this size is only as good as the people who run it from the bottom up." he pointed out. "We all work together as a team. Everyone has the common goal of making sure everyone has a good time, a good safe time while the ranch is actually being run. We take a great deal of pride in knowing that none of our visitors have ever had a serious injury."

Eli looked confused, "You can't both be boss. So who is the real boss?"

Rowdy chuckled, "That would be Beau."

"That's impressive." Ben said admiringly to Beau. "I understand you have a fairly constant stream of clients coming through here, yet the ranch runs smoothly and shows a steady profit.

"We've been real fortunate. The man that has steadily kept things going all these years even when Rowdy and I were keeping up with the rodeo circut is a man among men. Yancy Kincaid," he pointed at his friend, "Yancy is Rowdy's ol' man. He was my pop's best friend from the time they were kids. He stepped in as a father figure and mentor when my dad died."

"Sounds like you have all been blessed with an amazing individual." Drina answered. "You really are fortunate."

"That's kinda what Drina did for Kaylee and me after our folks died. She just sort of took over the parent part even though she really didn't have to." Kyle stated in a rare moment of seriousness. "I never really thought about it much before." He look at his twin, then at Drina. "You could of hired somebody to stay with us at home and kept on with your life, but you didn't."

"We didn't make it very easy sometimes either." Kaylee added. "I don't think we ever thanked you for that. For not just going on with your life I mean, and we were pretty little then too." Kaylee added.

Drina was moved almost to the point of tears. "I don't regret a single minute. I needed you two as much as you needed me. We needed each other. But, I don't think I could have done it without the band helping like they did. We all worked together, and I wouldn't change it. But, thank you I'm glad you like being with us. I know it isn't always easy."

CHAPTER SIX

**** "I really like all the side walks around here." Kaylee remarked, looking around. "I thought we'd be walking around in a lot of dust and mud."

Beau smiled, "Well, it actually was that way when Rowdy and I were growin' up. But, we put in the sidewalks and asphalt when my youngest sister was about four. It accomodates her wheelchair and walker so she can get around and be more independent. She was born with Spina bifida. My older brother, Brett, myself, Rowdy, Yancy and my oldest sister, Bobbi have all worked together to make things easier, more normal for her. We've taken care of her since she was born.

Eli looked confused and poked Ben in the arm and whispered, "What's....Spina...."

"Spina bifida," His step-dad whispered back, smiling down at the boy and gave a brief explanation of the condition.

"I think I've heard of it but I didn't know what it was." Then aloud he asked Beau, "Is that why she uses a wheelchair?"

"That's why," Beau answered easily. "She's usually in one of three wheelchairs depending on the terrain but she's learnin' to use a walker now. We encourage her to use it as her leg muscles strengthen. She's becoming quite the gad about." He added, smiling with pride.

"Putting all that around, that's a really nice thing for all of you to do. How old is she? Will we get to meet her?" Kaylee asked hopeful that there might be someone else close to her age to hang with.

The cowboy looked down at her, "I'm guessin' you ladies are about the same age. She's nine, be ten next month; and we like her to get out as much as she can. She's learnin' to do things around the ranch as her body strengthens and her balance improves. One of the things she does is to help Genny train by timing her barrel runs. Gen wants to be a champion barrel racer."

"Ooooh, I love watching that. The horses get so close to the ground when they're turning around the barrels. I'd be too scared to do it but it's very exciting to watch."

Beau opened the door and stepped back, allowing room for everyone to enter the indoor arena.

As soon as their eyes adjusted to the lighting both Eli and Kyle admired the wooden walkway that ran around the entire perimeter of the arena.

"You put this in too, so she can come in whenever she wants? It's really cool."

"Thanks, she seems to enjoy it. I think it does her a lot of good." Beau answered.

Rowdy continued, "She sure seems to be a lot more active and happier. Usually ends up on one of the platforms to watch whatever's goin' on in the arena. She goes up a ramp that curves around each one. She 'bout gave us a heart attack when they were first finished."

Yancy chuckled, "Did she ever! Little minx, she'd start at the top and roll down like it was a slide. Wouldn't apply the breaks till the last couple of feet. Whew! Sure was glad she stopped that. Darned near took my shins off several times till I threatened to turn her over my knee."

That brought a chuckle as the three men remembered and the new comers got an idea of Ava's spirit.

"Yeah I'm sure that threat really scared her into behavin'." Rowdy said as he clasped his father's shoulder.

Just then Ava's frantic waving caught Rowdy's attention. She pointed to the teen age girl and horse in the arena. The men looked and groaned when they recognized the horse Genny was riding - or trying to ride. They excused themselves and hurried over to where Ava was waiting on one of the elevated platforms.

"Hi, Tadpole. What in the blazes is she doin' riding that horse? She knows that stallion isn't ready to be worked with yet." Beau asked after kissing Ava's head. She hugged both men and kissed their cheeks as they squatted on each side of her chair.

"That's the one she came out with. I reminded her that you and Rowdy didn't want anybody messin' with him yet, but she wouldn't listen. She said she could handle him and wants to add his flash to her barrel routine, like that would help her score. She wants him to pick her, but I don't think he wants anythin' to do with her. Except for Kitt, he's the prettiest horse we've ever had." Both men nodded their agreement. She motioned to the group standing by the door. "Sorry to interrupt your time with the new people, but I was gettin' worried. He's not wanting to follow commands and then she gets rough with him and he misbehaves and then she loses her temper. I think it scares him when she yells. I thought...." She stopped and bit her lip.

"You thought what, honey?" Beau asked gently, wondering why she was reluctant to finish. He glanced at his friend who was also concerned at the change.

"You thought what? Whatever it is let's get it out and deal with it."

"I thought, I think maybe I saw her use a little stick or a whip to pop him a couple times. I mean, I'm not really sure....cause it kinda looked like it....but then it wasn't there. But right after, he would squeal and jump around and....he even reared once. I was afraid she'd fall off and get hurt. I told her not treat him so rough, but she just got snotty and said she knew what she was doin' and to mind my own business. I don't think he likes her."

"I'm not sure that horse likes anyone. But he has reason and she knows it." Rowdy added, frowning at the rider.

Ava glanced around to the group by the door. She grasped Beau's hand, "Dad, that girl looks like she might be close to my age. Do you think she'd like to be friend?"

Beau closed his eyes and savored the moment. He loved being called Dad, it felt so right. It was odd, he didn't feel that way about the other two. They felt like sisters, but....Ava was his daughter. The daughter of his heart. He kissed her hand and motioned the group over. "I think you and she are goin' to make great pals. You seem to have a lot in common. She reads a lot - like you. She's real smart - like you and spends way too much time alone - like you. They'll be here for three months so you'll have a lot of time to get to know each other."

When Beau introduced everyone Ava gasped, clapped her hands and squealed in delight. "Oh, I'm your number one, biggest fan in the whole world, Miss Skylard. I play your music every day and go to sleep with You're Forever In My Blood playing on my CD player all night. I've worn out two CD's already." Ava gushed.

"Thank you, Ava, but please call me Drina. I'm just here to help herd cattle and horses and be with the twins. But I think we have some cd's in the camper and we'll all autograph them if you want. We'll even have the rest of the band send you some signed CDs. Gotta take care of our biggest, number one fan."

"Absolutely!" Riley agreed with a smile as she shook hands with the happy nine year old.

As Beau had anticipated, the two girls hit it off at once. Within moments they were talking and laughing and separating themselves from the group to get better acquainted. They ended up on platform two where they were looking out over the arena, watching as Genny wrestled with the young Palomino Stallion.

"He's so pretty!" Kaylee breathed. "It doesn't look like they like each other very much." She noted.

"Rowdy doesn't think he likes anybody. He and my dad saved him from a man that was abusing him. When they brought him home, he was skinny and dirty and had fresh whip marks on his body. If you moved fast or made loud noises around him, he'd start jumpin' and buckin' and trying to break away. It was awful. His eyes always looked so sad." Ava answered.

"Oh, that's awful. I don't know why people do things like that. I hope that man was punished."

Ava smiled, "Oh yeah! Rowdy said dad beat the crap out of him. I wish I'd been there to see it."

"Good! I'm glad." A quiet moment later, "I don't mean to be nosy or anything but - did you call Beau your dad? I thought he was your big brother."

"Yeah, he is. I mean....he is my big brother, but he's more like my dad. My real dad was ashamed of me when I was born and my mom, I call her Lillie 'cause she doesn't want me to call her mom....Anyway, her feelings were hurt 'cause my birth dad got mad at her when I was born with problems. I guess she loved him more than me. She didn't want to take care of me, so daddy got guardianship of me and then he, and Bobbi, our oldest sister, and Brett, my oldest brother and Rowdy all took care of me instead. But it was mostly Beau and some nurses that did when he was gone. So you see, he's a lot more like my dad than my brother, and I wish he was."

"Wow. That's awful. I...."

"It's ok....I know what you mean. When Lillie's not around I can call him dad all I want and I think he likes it too. I like being with him a lot more than with Lillie. He wants to adopt me, but Lillie won't let him."

"I hope he can someday. Seems like he would be a great dad." Kaylee agreed. "Drina's our big sister and guardian too. She got guardianship a little while after our parents died in a plane crash. They weren't both her parents. We all have the same mother, but she had a different dad. He was a cop and got shot by a drug dealer. His name was Nicolaus. She liked our dad though. He was a good dad."

"My birth father also died in a plane crash." Ava said. A loud whistle caught their attention. Beau and Rowdy had gone into the arena and were waiting for Genny to meet them.

"Oh-oh. I told Gen they didn't want that horse to be worked with yet, but she got him out anyway. Ooooh, they're both mad. She's in big trouble now."

The girls looked at each other and giggled. Suddenly, the young stallion jumped and broke away from Genny dragging her several yards in the lose sawdust until she finally let go of the reins. He raised his head high, pranced around and whinnied like he was saying, "Na na naa na na." The girls watched the horse run around the arena kicking up his heels. He squealed as he ran around almost as if he were making fun of the girl.

Genny slowly picked herself up and glared at the horse as she began brushing the sawdust off her clothes. The men ran over to her, "Are you hurt?" Beau asked as he and Rowdy each held an arm to steady her. "If you're not, you're gonna be," he said angrily.

She glared at her brother, "I can handle him," she declared between gritted teeth. "He just needs to be taught a lesson and know who's boss." With that, she pulled a crop from her english riding boot and took a step toward the horse.

Rowdy grabbed the crop from her hand and broke it over his knee and threw the pieces at her feet. When Rowdy confiscated the whip, Beau grabbed her arm and pulled her back and around. "What the hell do you think you're doin'? No one, I repeat....no one uses a whip on or mistreats an animal on this ranch! Ever!"

"You use a bull whip!"

"To give commands to the cattle, never to use on them!"

"Whoa!" Whispered Kaylee. "I've never seen anyone try to whip an animal before."

"The only time I can remember seeing Dad and Rowdy this mad was when they caught some boys hangin' a cat from it's tail in the barn last year." Ava added.

Yancy whistled softly as he watched the drama unfolding in the center of the arena.

Tad, one of the riding instructors, (Former Marine) stepped up beside Yancy. "What's goin' on, Yance? Why the show?" Before the forman could answer, the younger man spotted the prancing horse who appeared to be paying more attention to the girls on platform two than anyone else.

"What's that psycho stud doin' out of his stall?....Gen wasn't tryin' to ride him was she?" he asked incredulously.

"Yup," The forman answered. "They're not hittin' it off very well."

Ben told his group quietly, "I think we should step out of the building. I don't think they would appreciate having an audience."

Yancy shook his head. "You're wrong, son; y'all have every right to be here. One of the founding ideas of this ranch is to teach the humane treatment and training of animals....and of the trainers." He pointed toward the young woman in the center ring, she knows better than to whip a horse. Been taught since she was put on one as a toddler. Don't exactly know what's goin' on in her head but she knows you don't take it out on an animal. She also knows that we are all on display here. While we go about our regular duties, we are representin' the core values of what the ranch is for and of Beau himself. We don't tolerate meanness of any kind."

———∿∿∿———

Kaylee watched in fasciation as the palomino pranced around the area, thoroughly enjoying it's new found freedom. She loved the way he held his head and tail high and the way the mane flowed in the air, almost like a flag blowing in the breeze. She was amazed at how beautiful he was when he pranced and pawed the sawdust and twitched his ears to catch all the sounds in the building.

He turned to face her and their eyes met. It was then that Kaylee felt the bond for the first time. 'Nugget.' She smiled at the stud that calmly made his way to his chosen partner.

CHAPTER SEVEN

**** Kaylee and Nugget were following Rowdy to the stables where she would begin her training as a horse owner. The rest of the group were following so they would know where all the supplies were kept. Kyle would also begin the process of meeting the available geldings and mares.

Beau had kept Geniveve behind and they were standing toe-to-toe outside the arena. He was not finished with his sister and she was furious with him.

"We distinctly told you that stud was not ready - that you were not to work him." He was fuming and walked a few feet from her as he regained control before facing her again.

"I can't believe you gave her my horse for her time here. Just gave him away, right out from under me!" Gen pointed to herself, "My horse, Beau! You gave my horse away to a complete stranger. You could tell she hadn't ever been on a horse before!"

Beau stood open mouthed, staring at her in stunned disbelief, as a baby blue Mustang Convertible came up the driveway and stopped a few yards from the siblings. A young blonde stepped out of the car; the huge smile on her face faded as she observed the stand off.

As she walked toward her siblings she noticed Yancy out of the corner of her eye. He held his hands palm down in a silent message to 'go slow, all is not well.'

She mouthed, 'Ok,' and 'Thank you,' before blowing him a kiss. He grinned, winked, and caught the kiss in mid air.

She grinned, glad to be home among normal people. As she neared her siblings she was amazed at the anger she saw in their faces. It was rolling off both of them.

"Your....horse? Since when do you decide a horse is yours just because, let alone one that clearly doesn't like you. And do you really think he'd allow you to work with him after you took a whip to him? An abused horse? Who are you?"

He turned and stormed away from her before he said something both would regret.

"Hi, Bobbi," he said after taking a few deep, cleansing breaths. "You picked a heck of a time to drive up. It's good to see you, honey." He said as he took his sister in his arms and kissed her forehead.

"It's ok, sounds like you need an arbitrator. What's goin' on?" She was looking back and forth between her older brother, and younger sister.

"Well," Beau said. "Are you gonna tell her or shall I?"

"What difference does it make, she'll take your side?" Genny shot back and turned back to the arena.

"Come back here, we are not finished." Beau said as evenly as possible.

The mutinus teenager stopped in midstep, crossed her arms and stomped back over to her older siblings.

"I'm not goin' to let this slide, Gen. It's too important for the family, for the ranch, for the animals. What you did is against the very principals of this ranch. I want to know where your head is, or more importantly, where your heart is?"

Bobbi raised her hands up. "Whoa, could we start at the beginning so maybe I can be of some help here, please?" The family attorney at work.

"Fine!" Geniveve fumed, "I was practicing in the arena and breaking in a new horse. Then Ava had to go stick her nose into my business and get everybody upset and got me in trouble. That's what!"

Genny stared at the ground, unable to meet Beau's eyes, which was not lost on Bobbi. "Ooo-kaaay. You were practicing with a new horse." Genny nodded, daring a glance at her brother. "What's wrong with your horse? Why did you choose to break in a new ride in the middle of the season?"

Genny glared at her. "See? I knew you'd take his side."

"Honey, I'm not taking any body's side. Right now I'm just tryin' to understand the situation."

"The situation is that Ava can't keep her mouth shut and everybody jumps when she cries wolf and I have been humiliated in front of clients and had my horse taken away from me and given to a little nobody for their time here." She huffed her frustration.

Bobbi glanced at Beau and raised her eyebrows.

He took a breath, "I don't know how this got so blown out of proportion, but....let's see. Number One. I did not give her that horse, he chose her! When she leaves he goes with her!" Genny's jaw dropped in shock, she began to argue, but Beau raised his hand to silence her. "I don't want to hear it, Gen! Those two are very good for each other. You were there....you saw as well as I did....The Bond, it's already there. Number Two. You already have a Bond with your own horse. Number Three. Ava knew you were having trouble, and she knew that horse was not to be worked. She also knew that if she had kept silent she would have been in trouble too. Number Four...."

"Whoa, ok. Back up a bit here." Bobbi held one hand up and held the other flat on top of her fingers in the standard 'time out' sign. "Exactly what horse are we talkin' about that isn't ready?" She asked.

Geniveve rolled her eyes. "Ok, fine, I know they said that stud wasn't totally ready, but he is so perfect. With his coloring and confirmation I would be way ahead of the game. I could get a lot of attention riding him."

Both of the older siblings were dumbfounded. Bobbi spoke first, "Gen, all I'm hearing is me, me, me. You didn't mention having a good reason to not be usin' your horse, you didn't say you had discussed this with Beau or Rowdy either one. You just chose a horse because of his color and the attention you would get? Tell me this is not the horse I think it is...."

She glanced at Beau who raised his eyebrows and nodded.

For several minutes Bobbi was speechless. She just stared at their younger sister. "Let's see if I understand this. You were riding the psycho stud? Geniveve, tell me you didn't?!"

"He's perfect, Bobbi! The judges would so be looking at him."

"Is that all you can think about? The judges, points, attention?" Beau was aghast at what he was hearing. He rubbed his hands down his face and shook his head.

"No one, no one takes a horse without checking with Rowdy or myself, you know that. You know both of us told you that stud was not ready, we gave you specific instructions not to even attempt to use him. You also know that no one takes a horse as their own without the knowledge and permission of myself, Rowdy or Yancy. You know this. The horse chooses it's partner! Both you and the horse are a team, one unit. We do not own our horses! We work with them. You've known this all your life." He let that thought sink in a minute.

"You also knew that particular horse had been badly abused and was untrusting. And more than anything else, you know that abuse toward animals, will not be tolerated on this ranch - by anyone. You....know.... this. You have no idea how long it took me to gain his trust. You have set his training and trust in me back months!"

Genny was staring at her boots now and Bobbi was the one staring open mouthed. "You hurt him? You abused a horse that had already been abused? Well?!....I'm waiting for an answer, Geniveve!"

"I didn't....hit him....hard, I barely even tapped him."

"You....barely....tapped him." Beau's face was entirely without emotion and his voice was cold and low, never a good sign.

Everyone knew that face and that voice meant he had reached his breaking point. "You grabbed that crop outta your boot like clockwork. You were biting nails to get at that horse. How long have you been usin' a whip, Geniveve?!" He turned away from her again, took his hat off and run his hand through his hair before replacing his hat. He looked at the sky and murmured, "Lord, if you really are up there, I could sure use some help down here before I muck this up. I don't know what to do. Please send me a sign, give me a direction."

As he turned back toward his sisters he saw Drina walking toward them. The sun was shining down and reflecting off her curly blonde hair and gold silk blouse, giving the illusion that she was bathed in light.

She was still wiping tears as she approached them, "I'm sorry to interrupt, but I may not get another chance any time soon." She looked directly at Beau, "I wanted to thank you for what you did. I haven't seen my sister so happy since before our parents died. She just kinda closed up after that and became afraid of everything. She wouldn't go near the horses, didn't want to be with people, she stopped coming out on stage with the band,...I have been so worried about her. But somehow, I have this feeling that we're going to be ok. I....I think God led us here to this ranch, to all of you so we could find ourselves again, so we could heal." She looked at each one of the siblings, smiled and wiped another tear and nodded. She grasped his hand and squeezed. "Thank you, thank you for giving me my sister back."

Genny stood looking at the songbird. "Both, of your parents died at the same time?"

Drina nodded, "Yes, they were killed in a plane crash. They were coming back from a business convention. My mom married Ken when I was about twelve I guess. He took me in just like I had always been his. My biological dad was a cop and was killed in the line of duty when I was ten. Ken really stepped up to the plate. I've tried to pinch hit for them, like he did with me, but sometimes I think I'm totally failing both of them." She shrugged and smiled briefly.

"Looks to me like you're doing a pretty good job." Bobbi said softly. She held her hand out. "I'm Bobbi, I'm the third B."

As the two ladies shook hands Beau came out of his trance. "I'm sorry, I don't know where my manners are. Bobbi, this is Drina Skylard. She and her brother and sister will be stayin' with us for three months. Ava and Kaylee have already hit it off. Ava is helpin' Rowdy show her how to bed her new horse down."

Genny roused then. "She....the palomino took to her right off. He went up to her on his own and ate out of her hand. He let her pet him and after a bit he let her ride him all around the arena. He did a lot better with her than he did with me. I....I guess he's better off with her. They can learn together and maybe help each other." She gave Drina a little smile, straightened her shoulders and looked at Beau. Her voice cracked when she said, "I'm sorry, Beau." Tears began streaming down her cheeks. "I won't do it again, ever, please don't be mad at me anymore."

He opened his arms and she melted into them and cried on his shoulder. He held her close as Bobbi and Drina quietly walked together to the stables. "It was the behaviors I was so angry with, baby. That is just not like you. You've got to tell me what's goin' on babygirl, we can work through it."

Genny shook her head and continued crying into her older brother's shoulder. "I miss him so much! Why....did he have to leave?" she sobbed, refering to her eldest brother Brett.

"I know, baby." Beau rubbed her shoulder the way Brett used to. "I know....I miss him also. He was doing his duty, and died doing what he believed in. He loved being a SEAL, he lived and breathed it. That was his job, he would have rather have chased after alqueida than a steer any day. He was proud of what he did and so am I. I have to remind myself of that everyday. It's what gets me through without him."

Gen looked up at him. "But, you came home. This is my first birthday with out him...."

'So that's it'....Beau nodded.... "Is that what this is all really about....?" His voice died away as Drina and Bobbi entered the stables.

———⁓ℳ⁓———

Drina studied the newest arrival. Bobbi was so pretty, about 5'5", with a hourglass figure. She wasn't big by any means, but was all muscle under that elegant three piece suit. Bobbi wore three inch heels, and a dove gray pin striped suit; she was the total package. Her light blonde hair was up in a tight bun, and her baby blue eyes sparkled with merryment.

Ava looked up from wiping down a bridle and a huge grin spead across her face. "Bobbi!" she cried out and raised her arms for a hug.

Her older sister beamed and lifted her into a firm embrace. "Hey, Tadpole. I hear you made a new friend today."

Ava nodded and waved her hand to Kaylee. "This is Kaylee. She's my new best friend...." Both girls began talking at once about how they had just clicked and felt as if they had known each other for ever.

"That's great, sweetie. I am so glad you've made a friend you can pal around with and write and call each other even after they leave. We'll have to see about getting the two of you together throughout the year."

"Oh, that would be awesome!"

"Wow! Really?" Came the answer from Kaylee.

"Well, I know how lonely you get and everybody needs a best friend." She looked at Drina. "Is that something that would be possible on your end? I'm sorry, I should have asked before I said anything...."

"No, no." Drina interrupted, "I think it's a wonderdul idea. Kaylee gets lonesome too. Kyle has Eli to pal around with so Kaylee is usually on her own or with we adults." She looked at the smile on her sister's face and in her eyes. "I'll do whatever it takes to see that smile more often."

As the girls were grinning at each other, "All right then we can talk about times and dates later."

"All right!" Both ten year olds exclaimed together.

⌇⌇⌇

"So, you tamed this beautiful boy, huh?" Bobbi said to Kaylee admiringly. "That's pretty amazing. Has anyone told you about his history yet?"

Ava shook her head, "There hasn't been time. It's all been like a miracle. I told her a little bit but not the whole story."

The girls proceeded to tell Bobbi how it had all come about, making her even more amazed. "That's incredible. We were worried that he wasn't going to tame down enough to be safely ridden. We certainly didn't expect him to trust anyone. I'm impressed."

"Why?" The twins and Eli asked.

Just then, Rowdy and Ben returned from the tack room. Rowdy came to a complete stop so suddenly that Ben ran into him. "Oh. Sorry, Rowdy."

Ben looked up to find what had attracted the other man's attention. Then he saw Bobbi. He looked from Rowdy to the beautiful blond and grinned.

"Ben, Riley," Drina said. "This is Bobbi, she's the third B. Bobbi this is my guitarist Ben, and his wife Riley." She waved at her best friend. "She's my fiddler."

Ben smiled, put his hand out and said, "Hi, Bobbi. It's nice to meet you."

She looked at Rowdy and then away making little eye contact. "Hi, welcome to the ranch. Hello, Randy."

Rowdy tipped his hat slightly and winced at the use of his given name. "Barbara." He said simply.

Drina and Riley looked at each other with raised eyebrows, and worked hard to hide a smile. There was something romantic going on between these two....whether they knew it or not.

Riley stepped closer to her best friend and whispered. "This is going to be a veeery interesting three months."

Drina nodded and whispered back, "Oooh, yeah."

The three ten year olds, and eleven year old, completely unaware of the sudden tension in the stable were looking from one adult to another. Finally, Ava shrugged and began telling the others about the horrible condition Beau and Rowdy had found the horse in.

"He was skinny and dirty and he had sores on him and cuts where the guy whipped him. It was awful."

"Wow," Kyle said looking at the horse. "You can't see anything now."

"That's because Rowdy and my dad took him to the vet before they even got him home. They had to give him medicine every day and it took about a few days to get him clean."

"Gee," Eli said, "Was he that dirty?"

Sensing this was more than just morbid curiosity, Rowdy took up the explanation. "Well, he had been badly treated for some time; kept in a filthy stall, he was whipped and starved. We had a hard time gettin' him to let us touch him much. We could only bath him a little bit at a time. Being touched really stressed him out. He was scared, nervous and didn't trust anybody, not even Beau - and he can win over any animal. He was afraid everybody that came near him was out to hurt him." He said as he petted Nugget's beautiful, smooth neck and scratched his ears. "He's come a long way, haven't ya fella?"

"What happened to the man that had him?" Kyle asked.

"Well," Rowdy said, "Let's just say that he wasn't feelin' real good when we left."

Ava grinned, "Dad beat the crap out of him," she said gleefully.

The boys were staring at Rowdy, mouths open, eyes wide.

Kaylee hugged the big neck and gently stroked his nose. "Thank you for saving him." She said and looked at him, her heart in her eyes.

"It was my pleasure, lil' miss" he said smiling.

CHAPTER EIGHT

**** Two weeks later, the 'dudes,' were finally going to get in on a round up. Though it was only for practice, they were all excited. Everyone, including Ava was going. Her hand made, customized saddle was finished and she had been practicing under the tutelage of Rowdy, (who had taken both girls under his wing). Both girls were throughly enjoying their horses and each other. When they weren't riding they were playing games, watching movies, listening to music, or timing Genny's practice runs.

Rowdy also found time everyday to work with Kaylee and Nugget, whom she had nicknamed Nugs. Ava watched and listened (and added her two cents worth as she saw fit) as Kaylee learned how to brush Nugget's coat, mane and tail. She learned the difference between the different brushes and curry comb and when to use each. She learned how to clean and care for his hooves; she talked to the vet about his continued medical care and was shown how to administer the medications, when a call to the vet was recommended and the regular care that horses require. Ava had been given the privilege of teaching her new friend how to care for the various parts of her new saddle and bridle that had been custom fitted to both herself and Nugget.

Kyle also had been taking riding lessons, though he thought that having ridden behind Drina on Odin had made him an accomplished rider. A few times of insisting he knew what he was doing and being spilled to the dirt anyway taught him otherwise. A spirited but well trained mare named Trixie had chosen him. At first he was appalled. While he liked her, it took all of ten minutes to get over the idea that his horse was, "A girl." He had quickly fallen in love with the beautiful, brown eyes, gentle mannerisms and fiesty spirit. He delighted in the picture they made with his new saddle, chaps and cowboy hat.

Drina had been taking videos with her Samsung Note three phone and let them see their progress from one day to the next. She also made sure she spent time with the twins individually and together. Having been touring ten out of twelve months of the year for the last three years the twins knew Drina more as a family acquaintance than as a sibling. The plane crash that took their parents changed all that and as a result of the ranch vacation, they were growing as a family. Kaylee was becoming less anxious and fearful more confident and independent. She was talking more and initiating conversations with more people, particularly Rowdy for whom she had developed a huge crush.

Not only was the ranch good for Kaylee, but she was good for the ranch; Ava in particular. Ava was willing to practice more with her walker, she was exercising more and as a result, was feeling better and growing stronger all the time. She was spending less time shut up in her room and had developed a tan for the first time.

Lillie was noticing the differences in her youngest daughter as well. She saw how hard Ava worked to improve and strengthen her body and how Kaylee would help with that exercise. She watched how Drina mothered her siblings, how she treated each with the same level of love and care. She noticed how Ava turned to Beau as a parental figure and how she had blossomed under his care, attention and praise. She seldom turned to Lillie. Seeing this had allowed her to understand and accept the truth regarding Brett, Beau and Bobbi's long time comments about the inequity of her treatment toward her three youngest daughters. She had slighted Ava from the day she had been diagnosed with Spina bifida and she was ashamed.

⁓⁓⁓

Riley, Ben and Drina rode along side a small herd of heffers, watching as Beau and the hands demonstrated how it was done. Drina stared as Beau stood in his stirrups, whistled and called instructions.

To their surprise he had a bullwhip that he used to give commands to the herd.

Not once did he use it on the animals. Drina was amazed with the precision, and skill with which he used it, watching this made clear the term, 'crack the whip.'

He reminded Drina of Jim, the main character in her favorite movies, (The Man from Snowy River, and Return to Snowy River). It wasn't physical, more of a spiritual resemblance. He cracked that whip and was just as skilled with it. She could picture Beau riding that black stallion across the Australian landscape. She grinned to herself.

Riley looked between both cowboy and her best friend. "Ok, Drina....admit it. You like him."

Drina looked at her friend in shock. "What?! You're crazy, I can't stand him. All we do is argue."

Riley laughed. "Oh, don't give me that! I see the way you watch him....you like that cowboy, chaps and all."

Drina shook her head. "No, Ri'....I can't stand him....He's bossy, annoying, conceited and egotistical, not to mention that he's a control freak extroidinaire...."

Riley interrupted. "And he's been kind, patient, sweet, considerate and good with the kids, great with animals, plays the guitar, the fiddle, and he's hot as hades." She grinned and laughed outright when Drina blushed bright red. "Honey, just admit it. You liiike, like him! We've been here for two weeks and you've been drooling over him like a love sick puppy."

Drina gave her friend a black look. "I have not! Drooling like a sick puppy, get real! You're way off, Ri'. Besides.... even if I did like him, which I don't. He doesn't like me."

Riley and Ben smiled knowingly at each other. "You just keep telling yourself that, honey."

⸺✺⸺

Kassi and her mother were packing a large lunch for the hands and their guests. It would be Kassi's job to drive the wagon out to the round up. As usual during this time of year Lillie had the weather channel on and was paying close attention as she worked. One of her jobs was to keep Beau, Rowdy, and Yancy notified of any major weather changes over the walkie talkie. Kassi froze when the anoying attention getting alarm blared. A severe storm warning was given, repeated and updated every fifteen minutes.

The young teen had been wanting to use the walkie all day so she grabbed it, stepped out of her mother's reach and and spoke into it. "Boss Man, this is Cowgirl One....Boss Man, this is Cowgirl One.... please respond? Over...."

A few seconds passed with nothing but static, then Rowdy's drawl came over the walkie. "Cowgirl One, this The Rowdy Cowboy....The Boss Man is tied up at the moment, can I take a messege? Over."

<hr />

Beau grinned at Rowdy and shook his head. Kassi always went undercover when she got to the walkie first and unbeknownst to her, Rowdy always helped that along.

"Cowgirl One, this is Rowdy Cowboy...."

<hr />

Lillie gave up reaching for the walkie and chuckled as she watched her daughter.

"Rowdy Cowboy, this is Cowgirl One. The weather channel has reported a severe storm warning and it'll be here in less than two hours....Over."

<hr />

That caught both cowboy's attention. "What are the storm details?" Beau interrupted after snatching his walkie back.

<hr />

Kassi frowned and stomped her foot as if her brother could see her. "Beau! You're not supposed to just ask like that! This is official." she added in her best school marm tone. "Now, do it right please."

—⁓⁓—

Rowdy pulled up beside Beau and Kitt, and didn't even try to hide his grin. Beau flashed him the frown of irritation because his younger sister wasn't available.

"Fine!" he said wearily, holding on to his temper. "Cowgirl One, this is The Boss Man. The Boss Man that can, and will turn Cowgirl One over his knee. What are the particulars of the severe storm? Over."

Rowdy couldn't help but laugh at the absolute silence that the walkie presented. Beau gave up and grinned at his friend. "Think that'll teach 'er?"

His friend, still laughing shook his head, crossed his arms to the saddle horn and leaned on them. "Nope." was the answer.

"Me neither," Beau added with a sigh his eyes laughing.

Finally, "Boss Man, this is Cowgirl One who is goin' to ignore Boss Man's attempt at intimidation." The men could hear Lillie's laughter in the background. Neither had heard the spontaneous sound in several years. It sounded good.

"Cowgirl One, this is The Boss Man. What kind of storm are we lookin' for? By the way, Cowgirl One. You forgot to say Over. If you're demandin' I keep up the protocol you have to adhere to it as well. Over!"

A full minute went by in silence. Finally, "Boss Man, this is Cowgirl One. The storm is supposed to include damaging winds, heavy rainfall, possible freezing rain and marble sized hail has been reported in areas it has already passed through."

Lillie took the walkie and continued, "The storm is in a line about a mile wide and will cut right through the center of the ranch, son. The way it shows up on the radar, it will hit the center of the ranch, all the houses, barns, stables, out buildings, and corrals. It looks like you'll be lucky to get all the animals and equipment in before it reaches us. Over."

"Ok. Thanks, mom. Cowgirl One, this is Boss Man, thank ya for the heads up. Need you to make sure everyone knows so all the families and buildings are battened down and prepared. We'll be busy gettin' all the cattle and horses out of danger so I need to know that I can leave that up to you ladies. Can I do that, Cowgirl One? Boss Man Out."

Beau could feel Kassi straightening her shoulders. "You can depend on me, Beau! Out."

Beau didn't have the heart to tell her she had forgotten the protocol again. Beau contacted his men by walkie and gave instructions to be carried out and knew it would be done.

Beau turned to Rowdy, "This is just what we need. A bad storm with a bunch of greenhorns. Ok, you go tell her majesty about this, an' that they need to hitail it back to the stables.... What in blazes are you shakin' your head for?"

"Sorry, bro. Di-rect orders like this have to come from you or pop, and seein' that pop's not here...." Rowdy worked hard not to grin at the dark frown on his friend's face and failed miserably. "Your rule, bro. Since that last client caused such a ruckus. Besides I think you need to practice your he-man and ro-mance skills."

"He-man and ro-mance skills? What the hell are you talkin' about."

"You need some practice at playin' nice with a certain female song bird. I don't need practice." He grinned and straightened in the saddle. "I already have the skills."

"My he-man and ro-mance skills are just fine." Beau said obstinately.

"Riii-iiight. That's why you go to so much trouble avoiding the prettiest client we've ever had and why you've gone all surley." Rowdy said chuckling.

"I'm not surley!" Beau growled. "What's wrong with you workin' on your he-man and ro-mance skills and tell 'er to get back to the ranch?"

"I don't need to 'cause I'm not stuck on anybody and you," he pointed to Beau's chest, "are....Oh yes you are, don't you go shakin' your head at me. You're crazy 'bout Drina, ya just don't want ta admit it."

Beau was shaking his head, "You're outta your ever lovin' mind, brother. The only thing I like about her are the kids. She annoys me to no end. She won't listen to anybody, thinks she knows everything about everything'. She's a high fallutin' little miss perfect that is as egotistical as a fe-male can get."

Throughout his friend's rant, Rowdy calmly nodded and smiled, "And she's got that great body...."

Beau closed his eyes visualizing Drina. "She's...." his eyes flew open. He looked at his friend with exasperation, horror.

Rowdy chuckled, "You are so far gone on this woman you might as well roll over and play dead. 'Caaause, you ain't foolin' anyone but ye'rself. You can shake your head at me all you want, but it won't change the truth."

He was laughing by now, pointing at his friend's heart again. "That there little lady owns ya heart and soul."

"I'm not talkin' about this any more. You are full of it, but I'll try to talk some sense into 'er if you won't, coward." In a rare fit of temper, Beau kicked his horse into a gallop but not before he heard Rowdy's full throated laugh following him.

Beau pulled Kitt up and petted his neck. "Sorry, about that, fella. That woman brings out the worst in me. Won't happen again, buddy." Then they continued on to the two ladies and Ben. He gave the hand up signal to stop and pulled up in front of them.

"We just got word there's a big storm front comin' through. The radar shows it to be a bad one. It's leavin' broken limbs, damaged roofs and injured animals. It comes with high damaging winds, heavy fast rainfall, freezing rain and hail the size of large marbles. I need y'all to get back to the ranch and stable your horses. Ranch hands will be comin' in with a lot of things to do in regards to their own homes as well as the ranch. So, if you all would take over carin' for their rides and stable 'em as they come in I would appreciate it."

"Of course, is there anything else we can do?" Ben answered.

Beau shook his head, "No, I just need the hands free to get the out buildings battened down and their homes prepared. So if you all would do that it'd be a big help."

Drina thought to herself, 'What a jerk, just taking for granted that we're incapable of pushing some cows around.'

Before she realized it she had already said, "That won't take all three of us. One of us should stay and help get the herd in."

Beau looked at her with a sigh of exasperation and pushed his hat up with one finger and thought to himself, 'I might have known she couldn't even let this one thin' go without an argument.'

"And just who would that one person be? There will be a dozen horses comin' in besides all of you and the little people. Don't you think that's enough? There are six of my men and Rowdy out here to get the herd in, and we know what we're doin' an' where they need to be put for safety. You don't."

When Drina started to interrupt Beau held up his hand. "All of you do however, know how to care for and stable a horse. If the hands have to do that somethin' will be left undone or the horses will be put in their stalls sweaty and possibly become ill because of it. This is a way you could be of help which is what this ranch is all about. Learnin' to work together for everyone's benefit including the animals. There will be plenty of time for you to herd cattle, believe me."

Ben stepped in, "He's right, Drina. I for one would not want to be out in this thing if it arrives sooner than expected. It's my understanding that cattle and horses can both spook in bad weather."

Beau nodded, "That's right. Even an experienced cowboy can be thrown and hurt by a panicked horse. Many a cowboys have been trampled by a stampede in just such a situation and I don't aim to get anyone hurt."

He looked at Drina as if expecting her to argue more and was surprised when she acquiesced, "I didn't think of it like that. All right, we'll take care of everyone's horses as they come in. Will there be a problem with your guys letting us do it?"

"No, Rowdy and I will contact them all with the walkie. They'll be glad to have them taken off their hands. Sometimes, their own families can be short changed when somethin' like this pops up." He turned Kitt's head, stopped and turned back to the three. "Thank you." He said simply, looking directly at Drina. Electricity zapped between the two before he turned and galloped away. Riley and Ben looked at each other and grinned at the dumbstruck look on Drina's face.

CHAPTER NINE

**** The storm turned out to be as bad as the weather channel had warned. Drina had expected resistance from the hands, but was pleasantly surprised when the horses were presented and the only thing said was specific likes or dislikes or needs of each animal.

The longer Drina was there, the more impressed she became with the total atmosphere and camaraderie of everyone who lived and worked on the ranch. The "dudes," were not treated as such unless they played the part consistently. The ranch ran like clockwork with everyone knowing their job and doing it. There were no laggers and no prompting unless an unexpected problem occurred which required a higher level decision. Drina was impressed with the respect the hands extended toward Beau and that it was returned. He carried his authority easily as did Yancy and Rowdy. She couldn't help but notice the respect and affection Beau clearly had for Yancy and Yancy for Beau. They did not have an employer - employee relationship; it was closer to that of a father and son, much like that of Rowdy and Yancy.

She caught herself wondering what it would be like to live here.... with him. But, as soon as she realized where her heart was taking her, she yanked it back. Live here - with him? She couldn't stand him.... didn't she?

When the wind and rain reached the ranch, they were ready and inside. Lillie suggested that they spend the evening with an old fashioned Hootenanny. The main house had a large room that was used for just such occasions. It was a huge room with two large fireplaces and plenty of wooden benches, rocking chairs, two rustic sofas and matching end tables. The furniture was all moved to the edges of the room and the rugs were removed to make room for dancing. Genny brought out her state of the art sterio and several others brought their personal musical instruments including The Skydivers. Lillie did herself proud and brought out dish after dish of her famous recipes. After the crowd roasted hotdogs, hamburgers and polish sausages in the fireplaces and polished off packages of marshmallows, graham crackers and pounds of chocolate bars for s'mores the music bagan.

Kassi, Genny and several of the ranch hand's daughters had been taking weekly dance lessons and were eager to show off their skills. Yancy produced some records and an old player that many of the younger kids had never seen and thought hilarious.

Gradually guitars, fiddles, harmonicas, spoons, snare drums, and a banjo were brought out and tuned, even Beau's Baby Grand Piano was opened up. With the wind blowing and freezing rain hitting the windows, the power went out. Though expected, the youngsters and guests from the city were relieved when the large generator kicked in. Hurricane lanterns and candles gave a soft, gentle glow to the house.

The Skydivers delighted in listening to the various musicians and were impressed with the talent that was displayed. As it turned out, Lillie told Drina that it was not unusual for several of them to get together. Living so far out, they had to make their own entertainment. It helped create the cohesiveness of the ranch. Drina danced with several of the hands and was delighted when Kyle and Eli both formally asked for a dance. Kaylee was in seventh Heaven when Rowdy bowed slightly before her, held out his hand and asked, "This lovely lady," for a dance.

Rowdy asked Bobbi next. She hesitated but took his hand and they danced slowly, arm in arm too, Drina's 'Our First Dance' played by Beau on his piano. Drina, Riley, and Ben were impressed with his skill. Beau watched as Bobbi lay her head on Rowdy's shoulder, and smiled to himself. 'It's about time.' He thought to himself. He was tired of watching them walk on eggshells with each other when it was more than obvious that they were in love.

Ava sat to the side and enjoyed watching the merriment and played the spoons as Yancy had taught her. Lillie brought out the starter violin she had originally bought for Kassi, but decided Ava would benefit from it more. Rowdy, and Beau had been teaching her to play their fiddles for the last few years. She took Ava into the dining room for the presentation. Beau noticed the two leave and was curiously concerned and followed. Ava was overjoyed with the small instrument and immediately turned to Beau and lifted the precious gift as he quietly entered the room.

"Look, Daddy! Lillie gave me a fiddle of my very own!" She didn't realize what she had said until the room had gone silent. Her face fell and her eyes filled with tears.

"I....I mean, Beau."

"It's alright, Ava." Lillie said looking from her youngest child to her oldest living child. "I understand." She smiled a little sadly. "I'm very, very sorry that I haven't been a better momma to you. But Beau makes a wonderful daddy, doesn't he?"

Ava bit her lip, but bravely nodded.

"I think that maybe if you still want to....we should see about making that official. Maybe I would make a better Nanna. Would you like that Ava...Beau?"

The instantaneous joy she saw on Ava's face told her she was finally doing right by her daughter."

When Beau started to speak, she held up her hand. "I've been thinking and praying about this a great deal lately. I think this is the best thing I can do for both of you. I don't know if you can forgive me, but honestly this is the best way for me to show how much I love you both. We can talk about the particulars later." she turned to Ava, "It's ok if you want to call him Daddy all the time now."

The big brown eyes filled with happy tears, "Really? Truly?"

Lillie smiled through tear filled eyes herself, "Really and truly."

"Oh, you are the best Nanna in the whole wide world. Thank you!"

Beau had to clear his throat twice before he could speak. "Are you sure about this, mom?"

"I'm very sure. I've been praying about it and I really believe I'm finally doing the right thing."

He nodded, looking away, looking at the floor, looking at her and finally, as a tear slid down his cheek he said, "Thank you." Then he squatted down next to Ava and asked, "Are you sure, Tadpole?"

"I'm the surest ever!" and threw her arms around his neck and found herself wrapped up in his big, strong arms. He knelt before his mother's wheelchair holding Ava when she turned and wrapped one arm around Lillie's neck and kissed her cheek.

Lora Cline's 'Sweetest of Dreams' swept through the house. Lillie kissed Ava and Beau and feeling lighter at heart than she had in years. "I think we're missing out on some great music aren't we?"

Beau put Ava back to her walker and placed her new fiddle and bow in the front basket and followed the child who would soon be his daughter into the front room. When Drina began to sing, 'Walkin' After Midnight', Beau picked Ava up in his strong arms and they danced among several other couples. When he put her back down on the little seat of her walker Ava said, "Everybody else has danced except you and Drina! Don't you think you should dance now?"

There were numerous, "Oh Yeah!"

"Sure thing!" and "Great idea!"

Rowdy, who had been playing his fiddle began, "The Montana Waltz," and grinned at Beau. Riley, Ben and Yancy took it up with their guitars and fiddle. When two other couples took to the floor and Kyle pulled Drina up out of her chair Beau knew he was had. They had been set up. He should be mad. He was mad! He was furious!.... wasn't he?

Drina shot Ben and Riley a murderous look that promised revenge. Then Beau took her in his arms and she forgot to plan the worst possible way to fire both of them.

Beau cleared his throat, "Ava asked me to see if you would give her some fiddle lessons while you're here. Rowdy and I have been teachin' her and she's doin' real good but she thinks it would be I'm quotin' here, 'cool beyond cool,' to have lessons from Drina.

"I'd love to! I usually give the kids lessons but since we've been here they've slipped. I could have them all together and they could help teach each other what they've learned. It would probably be good for them to see and hear the differences from different instruments and teachers as well. Would that be alright?"

"She'd love it. Kassi is usually her main playmate and the difference between a ten and fourteen year old seem to be growing. Thank you."

"It's my pleasure. It'll be fun for me too, she's a great kid. I couldn't help but notice that you both and your mom disappeared for a bit and.... and when you returned she had been crying. I'm sorry, it's none of my business. I wasn't trying to pry, I just...."

"No worries. Actually, you had a part in it so I guess you should know. Mom gave Ava a starter fiddle. She's been usin' mine and it's a bit big for 'her." He chuckled at her surprised look. "Yes, I have one and can actually play."

"So you play the piano, and fiddle. Any other information I should know about?"

"Guitar, and harmonica. Anyway, as it turned out....it's really amazing, mom has agreed to let me adopt Ava."

Drina fit in his arms perfectly, He rested his chin on the top of her head, oh yes. She fit so perfectly. Good thing she loved the high life, on the road all the time, different city everynight. She'd never be satisfied living on a ranch, too far away from....everything. Too slow, too few fans. Besides, soon he would have a daughter to raise plus the ranch to run. No, like Drina he definitely had too much on his plate to think about a serious relationship. Funny how well her and those great kids just fit into the ranch routine. 'NO, NO, NO!' He had to stop thinking that way. Besides he didn't even like her.... but she felt sooo good in his arms.

Why or why couldn't Ben and Riley mind their own business? She didn't want to dance with Beau Blanton - much. It would help if his arms didn't feel so warm and strong, yet gentle and safe. Her head fit under his chin just perfectly. Like a couple of puzzle pieces, they just felt right. 'No, No, No!'

It couldn't be right! He lived in the middle of nowhere - all the time. He had and liked having people and animals for which he was responsible. Besides, her band depended on her and she had the kids to raise. She had to find a way to make a home for them and still keep up with her career make a living. Yes, it had to be right for the kids, she had to put them first. Yes, that would help when she started thinking about how good it felt to be held in his arms, how well they moved together - as one.

Riley and Ben grinned at each other and winked at Kyle and Kaylee. Ok, the bait had been put in the trap, the mice were being drawn to the bait and the trap was set. Oh, this was going to be good! Both wanted the bait, (each other) and both were denying themselves with every excuse in the book. What fun it was watching them come up with reasons to dislike each other.

He cleared his throat, looked away and steered them into the next, empty room. As in the other rooms, several candles and hurricane lamps provided a soft even romantic light. "It's something that I've wanted to do for a long time. Rodney, the three younger girl's father was a real piece of sh--uh, work. A piece of work. I'm not sure how he so completely pulled the wool over mom's eyes but he did. Anyway, he got it in his head when it became obvious Ava had problems that she wasn't his. He accused mom of bein' unfaithful and gettin' pregnant by another man. His excuse was that he couldn't possibly have an imperfect child. Mom was hurt on so many levels, but instead of getting angry with him, she turned her anger on Ava."

"Oh my God! What kind of inhuman monster was he? She's a wonderful child. How could they have turned their backs on their own baby?" She asked appalled.

He smiled, delighted for some reason at her immediate response. "I've asked myself that a million times," he said shaking his head. "He wasn't satisfied with anythin' about the ranch except every penny he could get his hands on. Anyway, mom was unconsolable, I wonder sometimes if post pregnancy depression might have played a part in it. But, it's gone on for years. Brett, my older brother, Rowdy, Bobbi and myself took care of Ava. I hired a nurse to step in when one of us weren't here or when her medical needs were beyond our knowledge and skills. She's always felt more like my daughter than my sister and she's always thought of me as a father and mom as a grandmother."

"May I ask why it's taken so long for legalization to come into it then?" Drina couldn't fathom a mother turning against her own child.

Beau frowned as they continued dancing despite the old Steven Reeves hit, "He Just Needs To Go," was now being played. Neither noticed anything how it felt to be in each other's arms.

"For some reason, mom would never give up her paternal rights. Rodney died in a plane crash about eight years ago. At least Ava was too young to understand. I guess somewhere deep down, she loved Ava and just couldn't give her up. But, she was never a mother to her either. They don't have a Mother-daughter relationship, sheee said she's been watching how you are with Kyle and Kaylee, that you treat them equally. She realized she didn't do the same with the girls. She said she'd been praying about it a lot and felt that letting Ava go was the best, fairest thing she could do to make up for all the years of neglect. So, for the part you played in that....thank you."

Drina was touched to tears. "If I played any part in it, then I'm thankful."

All either could think of then was how good they felt in each others arms; how magical the room had become and how wonderful it was to just be together.

They couldn't look anywhere but into each others eyes. For some reason, his head was being drawn down closer and closer to hers. They didn't know what was pulling them together, but their kiss was so sweet, so right, so absolutely perfect.

Suddenly, the electric lights filled the room with impossibly bright lights and there were shouts of relief and joy throughout the house. Surprised, they broke apart and stared at each other a moment.

'What had they been thinking?'

"Well, anyway thanks for the help with Ava and....um,....for the dance."

"Uh, yeah, sure, that's ok. I'm....I'm glad I could help. Um,....I'd better find the kids and get them back to the cabin. Good night."

"Night." he answered gruffly.

CHAPTER TEN

**** "Hey, Drina! Get up! You gotta see this!" Kyle yelled as he and Eli rushed into their new winter clothes. Kyle and Eli wanted to beat each other outside so they could be first to stomp through the icy grass and slide on the driveway. So intent were they to get out first that for a few seconds they were stuck in the doorway, fighting to get through.

"Come on, Drina!" Eli called, "It really looks like they show it in the movies! Cool, huh, D? Can I call mom and Ben so they can see it too?" The boys were stomping around the yard, listening to the icy crunch under their boots. They slipped and slid their way to the driveway which was a solid sheet of frozen rain. The boys looked at each other and grinned as they ran and jumped on the slick surface fully expecting to slide gracefully down the length of the driveway. They slid all right. Their feet slid right out from under them and they flew down the slight decline on their rears.

Kaylee and Ava were watching the boys from the large window of Beau's home which over looked the main house and several of the guest cabins.

At first, the girls were just staring at the boy's antics. They both squealed and burst into laughter when the boys slid, turning and twisting as they tried unsuccessfully to slow their progress until the driveway leveled out.

The girls were laughing hysterically at the two boys. "Boys are sooo wierd." Kaylee said.

"Do boys always act and do wierd things like that?" Ava had brothers, but they were grown and she hadn't been around the ranch hand's sons much.

"Yeah, pretty much," Kaylee answered. "They go from being wierd to silly and just plain embarrassing."

Just then, the sun broke through the clouds bathing the ranch in a bright light that made the ice sparkle and glow. Kaylee, being from the South had never seen an icy yard and was mesmerized. "Oooh, it's so pretty. Everything looks like it's covered with diamonds and glitter." She pulled her phone out of her pocket and started taking pictures and sending them to Drina. She looked at her new friend, "Does it do this every year here?"

Ava smiled and nodded. "It snows a lot too, looks like a winter wonderland sometimes. Dad thinks I might be able to get out in it a little this year and maybe even help make a snowman." She grinned, "I can't wait."

"Cool, I hope it snows while we're still here. I've never seen snow, except on tv and Christmas cards. Wouldn't it be great if we could make a snowman together?" The thought excited them both.

"Daddy! Wake up! Come look at these boys, they...." giggle, giggle.... "they slid all the way down the driveway!"

Beau looked at his bed side clock. Six am. Crap! He'd over slept. Normally he was up and out by five o'clock. He smiled when her heard Ava's call and called back. "Yeah, ok baby. Give me a minute."

He looked bleary-eyed around the room. He was tired, almost felt like he had been on a bender but had only had a couple beers last night. No....it wasn't beer that had kept him from sleeping, it was that little songbird. Drina. More than that it was the way she smiled, that little dimple in her left cheek. It was the sparkle in her eyes when she laughed with her brother and sister. It was the way she was with his little Ava. God! She was so good with Ava. But, even more, it was the way she fit in his arms. She was so soft and warm and smelled like....what? A rose garden. And he could have kissed her all night.

'What? Where the heck had that come from? He couldn't be thinking like that! She'd be leaving in a couple months, she has a career that's all important to her and two kids to raise. Besides, he had a ranch to run, he had missing cattle to find or find out what happened to them. He had a child now, a child of his own. Or she will be as soon as the adoption is complete.'

He stumbled into the bathroom and looked into the mirror. Then splashed cold water into his face.

"Daddy! We're hungry!"

He looked in the mirror and smiled.... 'Daddy'. He splashed more water on his face. His daughter and her little friend were hungry. 'Could life get any better? Well, if he had Drina in it too - NO! No, he couldn't think like that. Be satisfied. Ava. Concentrate on Ava and the ranch.'

"Wow! That was cool." Eli was grinning. "Think we could do it again, maybe after we warm up?"

"Yeah, but the warm up first. I didn't know ice was so c-c-cold. Well, at least not the big stuff anyway." Kyle complained as they trudged back to the cabin, slipping and sliding until they gave up and walked in the grass.

"Hey, Drina. You up yet? We're hungry....and cold. Did you know ice outside was cold?"

The boys hurried out of their damp outer clothes and headed for the kitchen, rubbing their hands together.

They ran to stand in front of the fireplace, hands outstretched toward the warmth. "Ooooh, this feels sooo good." Eli soaked in the warmth.

"Yeah....good and warm. Drina! We're hungry! Can we have french toast? Please?" Kyle yelled to his sister.

"Yeah, yeah ok guys. I hear ya, give me a minute, I'll be right there." Drina hadn't slept at all. 'No, that wasn't right. She had slept, but....she had dreamed all night.' Sweet, beautiful, disturbing dreams of Beau Blanton. She had never met anyone like him before. She had dated a number of guys, but none of them had made her dream of them all night. She closed her eyes and pictured him, all six feet one inch of him.

Just as an experiment she tried to think of the other guys she had dated. No matter how hard she tried to picture them, their faces were always blurred and turned into that gorgeous cowboy.

"Get your head on straight D girl. Get him out of your mind. Like Mitsy Gaynor in South Pacific. Yeah. Just 'Wash that man right outa my hair.' She sang the song with a flourish and a two-step into the bathroom in an attempt to add energy and enthusiasm. She collapsed on the stool and sighed. 'If only it were that easy. But....it didn't work for her either.'

"Girl, you are in so much trr-ou-ble!"

<hr/>

"Get whatever games or things you guys want to use for a while together. As soon as the breakfast dishes are done we'll be going over to Beau's house." Drina told her brother and Eli.

"How come?" Kyle asked around a mouthful of French Toast.

She raised her eyebrows, "Excuse me?"

He colored at being caught forgetting his manners. Swallowing, he asked, "Why are we going over there? Why can't we stay here?"

"Thank you, Beau and Rowdy have to meet with Yancy about some important ranch business and it's not that safe for Ava to be out in this kind of weather yet."

"Oh," Both boys said together. "I guess she has a hard time getting around sometimes huh?" Eli asked.

"A hard time indeed, yes she does." she answered. "Apparently she had surgery a couple months ago and is just beginning to feel some positive results from it. Hopefully, at some point she'll be able to use crutches part of the time, but that's about as good as it'll get for her."

"Wow," Kyle added, "bummer. She doesn't act like she's sad or mad or anything."

"No, she doesn't does she? She seems like a very stable little girl."

"Must be cool living here, specially with Beau. Wow. How cool is that?"

"Yeah, awesome." His friend agreed.

Drina sighed, "Yeah, awesome," she murmured with a dreamy look on her face. She realized the room had gotten quiet. When she opened her eyes she found both boys looking at her, eyebrows raised.

She cleared her throat then folding the dish cloth she said brightly, "Ready?" And left the kitchen and their questioning looks as soon as possible. "Get a grip!" She told herself sternly.

***

Rowdy cleaned his boots in the mud room, knocked on the door twice and walked into Beau's living room after winking at the girls through the big window. Ava made her way over to him with her walker, a huge smile on her face.

"Well look at you, Tadpole! You're gettin' around like a regular speedster with that thing." He exclaimed as he knelt down, set her on his knee and gave her a loud kiss and hug.

"I know, right?" She said grinning and returning the hug and kiss. "Aren't you going to hug Kaylee too? She's been helping me practice walking. I can use the crutches a little now. My arms get tired but she's helping me to exercise to." Then proceeded to flex her arms he-man style, showing off the tiny bicep muscle she was beginning to develop.

"Really?" Rowdy said as he felt the precious little arm. He looked at Kaylee with respect and admiration, and smiled as she blushed. "Well I definitely have to give you a hug then if I may. You have hidden talents Kaylee the cutie, come on over here." He said and motioned with his free arm. She grinned and shrugged shyly and was immediately wrapped in his other arm when she moved to his side. He kissed her cheek and hugged both girls.

"Thank you for helping little Tadpole here." He said seriously, "You've made a huge difference in her life and we all appreciate it."

"Hey, Rowdy. Can you give her a nickname like me?" Ava asked hopefully, she looked at Kaylee and grinned. "He gives the best nicknames and only gives them to special people." She said.

"Hmm. A nickname for Kaylee the cutie. Well, she's certainly earned it hasn't she, Tadpole?"

"Hmmm," he looked Kaylee thoughtfully, "I know! What about Chickadee? It's this beautiful little bird that everyone wants to lure to their feeders." He looked at both girls.

"I love it!" Ava said clapping her hands. "What do you think Kaylee? Do you like it too?"

Kaylee's smile lit the room, "I think it's beautiful. Will you really call me that?" She asked Rowdy hopefully.

"I'd be proud to if you'd let me." He answered and gently kissed her forehead.

"Hey, bro! Get you hands off my ladies! You tryin' to steal 'em right outa my own home?" Beau stood in the kitchen doorway legs spread, hands on his hips and looking outraged.

Rowdy winked at both girls and told his friend as he steadied Ava back to her walker. "When ya got it, ya got it, bro. You just keep practicin', you'll get there."

There was the sound if stomping and laughing on the mudroom floor followed by polite knocking. Beau opened the door to find Drina and the boys.

"Thanks for comin' over on such short notice, Drina." He said, stepping back so they could all enter.

"Not a problem. You said it is an emergency meeting." Drina immediately went to Kaylee and hugged her ferociously. "Did you have a good time, honey? I thought you would. This was your very first sleep over." Drina noted the happiness in her sister's face and felt a lump in her throat. She looked at Ava and hugged her as well.

"I've had the best time ever! And I have a real nickname now!" She announced hugging her sister hard. "Thank you for letting me stay, Drina. I wish we could live here forever."

"Me too!" Ava agreed, it's almost like having a sister." The two girls looked at each in complete harmony.

Surprised at the instant thought of how nice that would be, Drina looked at Beau who had over heard. He smiled wistfully and for a moment, no one else was in the room until Kyle complained about the cold.

"Um, Nathan Medows, the head of our ranch security will be dropping his boy off in a bit if that's ok, Drina. His mom is our ranch vet and she's on call with a horse today and couldn't take him with her."

After blinking a few times to regain her equilibrium, she answered, "Of course, that's fine. How old is he? Is everything alright?"

"He's seven, and I hope so." He answered as he put on his coat and hat.

"Where's the horses?" Eli asked looking out the window.

"We're usin' the wheelers today." Rowdy answered, "Give the horses a break."

Beau and Rowdy took their coats and hats off in Yancy's mudroom and hung them on the pegs beside the door, they entered the house through the kitchen door, and Beau placed the box of doughnuts and assorted other breakfast goodies (from Lillie) on the table while Rowdy filled two cups with fresh coffee and took them to the table.

Yancy finished his conversation, hung up the phone and said, "Sherlock will be joining us in a few minutes. He said he has some interestin' videos and pictures from his surveillance cameras. Don't know exactly what, his boy was there and he didn't want to say it outright. He intends to drop Troy off at your place to spend some time with Kyle and Eli while we're talking."

"He couldn't give you any idea of what he found?" Beau asked.

"Nope, just that we are gonna want to see it and he wanted us all together." The foreman answered. "Mmm-mmm, these look good." And took a huge bite of a fresh bearclaw and washed it down with lukewarm coffee. He grimaced and was about to get up when Beau pushed him back in his chair.

"I'll get it, pop. You enjoy your breakfast," and replaced the cold coffee.

Yancy leaned his chair back and retrieved a new laptop from the counter and began setting it up. Both of the younger men sat staring as Yancy set the computer up for viewing.

"I....don't....believe it." Rowdy said grinning and winking at his life long friend. "Do you see that, Beau. Our pop here has a laptop."

"Mmm." Beau took a sip of his stong black coffee, and nodded. "And it looks like he even knows how to use it. Amazin'. Isn't it?" Both the men chuckled.

As Yancy flushed, (which added to their enjoyment) he gave them both a dark look. "Neither one of you boys are too big for me to take ya out behind the woodshed." He threatened, scowling.

"Now....now, pop. Don't get all lathered up. We're just surprised that's all. I never could get ya to even try my computer." Rowdy cajoled as both he and Beau worked to keep their faces straight. Rowdy looked closer at the machine. "This is a top of the line outfit, dad! I'm impressed. You must have studied up on different types."

Yancy got busy tearing his bearclaw apart and refused to look at them. Finally, he cleared his throat, "Lillie gave it to me for my birthday and the girls have been teaching me how to use it. They say I need to know how to get around on one and do things online," he said blushing even deeper.

"Lillie, huh?" Rowdy asked grinning. "You say thank you with some roses or a box of candy."

"Lillie prefers mums and carnations and don't eat candy much." He stopped his cup halfway and set it back down, took a deep breath and looked up with a scowl. "Now look...."

"Pop," Beau, who had known about the gift when Lillie was thinking about the purchase, said grinning. "It's ok. I couldn't be happier, for both of you. I actually like the idea."

All three looked up at the three hard knocks at the door.

"Saved by the knock." Rowdy said grinning and grasped his father's shoulder affectionately.

Fifteen minutes later the men were watching a surveillance video taken last week which coincided with a half dozen head of cattle coming up missing.

While Nathan Medows (former army ranger from Beau and Rowdy's team) found the desired video, he set the scene. "As you know, we've all been seein' more than the usual signs of wolves." The other men nodded. "I've been noticing more than that though." He took a packet of pictures from his pocket and set them in front of Yancy.

"My son Troy has been takin' pictures all over the place. His teacher gave the kids an assignment of sorts to work on over the summer, and winter. She's encouraging the kids to learn about the wildlife that shares the land. Anyway, Troy started seeing different kinds and sizes of footprints. He's been spending a lot of time online researching paw prints and matchin' them according to size, shape, claw position and such. Done a real good job. You'll see what I mean."

As the pictures went around the table the mood became more serious. Beau looked at the 3B's head of security, "You're sure about this? This is....I don't even know if Montana has ever had....damn! Timber wolves!?"

"Yeah." Sherlock said, "Bigger, stronger, meaner, smarter and far less timid than your average wolves. I've been telling the hands not to go out alone and no kids are supposed to get out of sight of their homes, just for safety sake."

"That's good, Nate," Yancy praised. "We may need to start spreading that around the entire ranch and every saddle, ATV, truck and/or jeep needs to have a loaded shotgun or rifle in it, and it wouldn't hurt for dogs to be penned or housed at night."

"I thought so too. I also think all hands needs to be packin' any time they're away from the main complex. Umm, we'll need to be extra careful with the guests. Some of them like to wander on their own...."

"You're right, Nate." Beau agreed and rubbed his hands down his face. "Ok. What ya have found for us?"

The four men watched several videos and bacame more concerned with each one. The last was watched several times.

"I don't believe it! I just don't believe it!" Yancy stormed. "I've lived in Montana all my life and I've never seen this kind if thing."

"Me either." Nate agreed. "I'm from Nevada, and I've never seen or heard of anything even remotely like this. I've been checking with some other people who have lived around and they say the same thing about the animal and the behaviors. Neither has been seen. I've also checked with some wildlife experts. None of them have heard of entire packs being trained like this."

"I can't believe the size of them." Rowdy breathed. "They have to stand at least four and a half feet at the shoulder! Good grief! They're body is larger than a good sized man's torso They're twice the size of a normal full sized wolf, look at the comparison. It looks like a horror movie animal."

Their boss shook his head in shock. He also was amazed by the animal's size, but mostly by the way the wolves took orders from the horsemen. "I take it we're the only ones to have seen this so far." Beau asked of his Head of Ranch Security, although he knew the answer.

"Of course. Although, we're goin' to have to make the Sheriff aware of it. I haven't heard of anything similar from other ranches, but we just found out so...."

"Ok. Nate, what's your professional recommendation?" Beau asked.

"Well, I think we need to encourage all the other ranchers to set up some surveillance cameras in places where they seem to be losing cattle. It may not be widespread, but everyone has lost cattle in some numbers. We have to make the other ranchers and farmers aware of this. We can't risk someone gettin' caught out by one of these things unaware. Just one would tear a man apart....and they don't travel alone."

The men agreed and watched the videos once again. No matter how many times they watched the sight of timber wolves working together to herd cattle to a specific area boggled the mind. It was decided that Beau and Nathan would take the videos to the Sheriff that afternoon and see how she wanted to handle notification of the ranchers.

CHAPTER ELEVEN

Four weeks later-

**** "Why couldn't they stay till after my birthday or why couldn't they have left Eli here?" Kyle asked for what seemed like the hundredth time.

"Kyle! We've been over and over this so often I'm getting whiplash." Drina said, beginning to lose patience. Ben, Riley and Eli had returned to their farm a week ago and Kyle was at a loss without his constant buddy.

"Ben's attorney got their court date moved up. There was no way they were missing out on this chance, you know that."

"I knooow. I just....I'm bored. Things are just more fun with him around."

"You mean you have double the brain power to think of mischief to get into," Drina said dryly.

Kyle flopped down on the sofa. "It's not fair!"

"What's not fair?" Drina sighed and put the pen down, knowing there would be no more song writing today, and it had been going so well. She had been getting so much work done, quality songs! She was beginning to think about extending their vacation and putting more effort into song writing and easing out of full time performing, just writing songs, recording and doing an occasional concert. That would allow her to get the kids off the road and give them a more stable home life. Things had been going so well on the ranch. Well, at least until Eli had left. They had finally got on the court docket for Ben to adopt Eli. Ben had wanted to give Eli plenty of time to get used to them being a family before introducing the idea of adoption. They were scheduled to stand before the judge later today. She couldn't wait to hear how it went.

"What's really behind all this, Kyle? I know you wouldn't have Eli miss out on having Ben as a dad so what's going on....really?" Drina sat beside her younger brother and just waited.

"We always spend our birthdays together. Ever since we were little," (Drina had to work to hide a grin at that).

"How can I have my birthday without my best friend?" He asked plaintively.

The light bulb went on. "I see," Drina didn't know why she hadn't thought of this before.

"You know, you can be best friends with someone you don't see very often. Just because you aren't together doesn't mean you aren't close. This should give you an idea of how it's been for Kaylee all this time. You've always had Eli to pal around with and she's had no one, but us."

"Uuuuh!" Kyle flopped back against the sofa back. "I know, but...."

"But nothing, Buddy, life is changing all the time. We have to change with it. Look how our lives have changed just in a year."

He sighed, "I know. Ben's gonna be a great dad and Eli really likes him. They're gonna be doin' a lot of guy stuff together now. And I'm really glad about that, I am. I know what it's like to have a dad and Eli doesn't. They're gonna have lots of fun."

"A lot of fun that you'll miss out on." Drina observed.

"You make me sound like a spoiled brat." He complained, sneaking a peak at her.

"Weeeell," she said. "What's something you think you might like to do on your birthday since you can't be with Eli?"

"Anything?" He asked.

"Well, within reason. What's your idea?"

"I'd like to hang out with Beau and Rowdy." He said enthusiastically. "That would be totally awesome! I really like them, they don't treat me like a little kid and they're always showing me how to do something that's really cool and don't make fun of me when I don't know how to do something."

"Wow. That's quite a ringing endorsement. You know, I can't say yes to that. That's up to them, but if you're serious, I'll ask. But, you have to remember," she cautioned when he looked ready to jump for joy. "They're busy, they have a lot of responsibilities and there may be things that you can't do or places they can't take you."

"I know, I'd be good and I wouldn't whine or beg, but that would be beyond cool."

The surprise birthday party for the twins and Ava, (who from that point on became known as the triplets) went off without a hitch. All three of the kids thought preparations were for Ava's party as her birth date was three days prior to the twins. Little did any of them know that it was a grand celebration, not just for their birthday's, but for all the kids had done and achieved individually and together.

As the party was winding down, all the gifts had been opened, but nothing had been said about Kyle's special wish. He was disappointed until he looked around at all the new friends they had made since coming to the ranch. Drina looked better than she had in a long time. She laughed and looked rested and....happy. When she smiled, her eyes smiled too, it wasn't just a stage smile anymore.

Kaylee talked and laughed more and didn't spend all her time in books anymore. He liked palling around with her and had found that she was more fun than he knew a sister could be. They talked, played games, rode their horses and sometimes Ava rode with them. He wished they could just live on the ranch and not go back on the road. They had been attending church with many of the ranch residents and Drina read the Bible to them before going to bed. They prayed together as a family and life was just....good.

He turned when a big hand clamped onto his shoulder. "Hey there, Cisco." Beau said smiling. "You look like you're doin' some serious thinkin'."

"Yeah," Kyle answered. "I was just thinking how great this party has been and....how much I love it here, and that I wish we didn't ever have to go home."

Beau and Rowdy smiled. "I think he needs to be put in charge of advertisin'." Rowdy said.

"I think you're right. That's about the nicest thing anyone has ever said about the ranch, Kyle. I can't tell ya how much that means to me, to all of us."

He pulled an envelope from his shirt pocket. "Rowdy an' I have one more thin' for ya." And handed it to Kyle. "We hope you like it, cause we're sure goin' to."

Kyle found a card inside showing several cowboys around a campfire. One was playing a guitar, one a harmonica and they were obviously singing. It said that while cowboys might come from different families they were all brothers of the heart. Inside was an invitation for Kyle to spend four days with them on the range as 'one of the guys'.... as a brother of the heart.

Kyle opened his mouth but nothing would come out. There was a huge lump in his throat and his eyes burned. When he tried again to speak (unsuccessfully) he gave up and threw his arms around Beau's waist and buried his face against his hero's wide chest.

Rowdy chuckled and as Beau wrapped his big arms around the thin shoulders, he said in a gravely voice, "I think he's acceptin' our invitation."

Kyle's head nodded vigorously against Beau's chest and he backed up just long enough to wipe the tears from his face before hugging Rowdy.

"This is the best present ever," he said smiling. "When do we leave?"

"Tomorrow mornin'. We've got some fencin' to check and cattle to bring in. Now," Beau placed his hand on Kyle's shoulder to impress the importance of what he was going to say next. "This isn't all goin' to be fun and games. Workin' out on the range is hard and it'll probably get cold. You'll need to stay with us at all times. *You need to understand this, Kyle. We're not expectin' trouble but we're missin' some cattle and need to check it out and we have been seein' signs of wolves.* They're generally more scared of humans than we are of them, but no chances will be taken. This is the best way to do it. Are we clear?"

"Clear. I'll stay with you all the time, I'll pull my weight and I won't whine or cause any trouble, you can count on me, I promise."

"Ok. Let's go tell your sister what all you'll be needin' then." And the three went in search of Drina.

"I'm not sure about this, Beau. He's only eleven and...."

"And there'll be twelve of us men. We'll take care of him, Drina.... trust me." Beau said looking intently into her eyes.

"I do trust you. More than you know."

"And you can trust that we'll get him back in one piece and he'll enjoy bein' one of the guys. We won't let anythin' happen to 'im." He almost caressed her cheek with the back of his fingers but thought better of it. His world was good, it was bright and warm and it had a future.... and he wanted that future to include a prickly little songbird as well as his little Ava, Kaylee and Kyle. He hadn't allowed himself to think of his life in terms of blessings in a long time, but he could clearly see that this tiny woman was one huge blessing. He wished he could depend on her becoming a permanent fixture in his life, but there were too many things standing between them. The main being that he knew she didn't feel the same.

⚬⚬⚬

They had been on the range for two days, the best two days of his life. Kyle looked around at the men as they worked to free the cow and her calf from a pen like trap. There were men on horseback with rifles or shotguns across their laps, looking, watching. Kyle sensed the difference in the atmosphere. The men were wound tight, they were alert....for what he didn't know but he wasn't scared. He felt safe in the midst of so much self assurance and confidence.

Then....he heard, what? It wasn't the wind, it was....in the wind. It sounded almost like the growl of a demon dog in a horror movie he and Eli had secretly watched. He'd had nightmares for a week.

"Beau," he said quietly, trying hard to not sound scared.

"Yeah, what is it, Kyle?" Beau answered not looking up from fighting with the trap. Rowdy pulled on the opposite side as they worked to free the Belted Galloway and her calf.

"I....I'm hearing something....it's behind us, I think."

"You think?" Rowdy questioned.

"Yeah, boss. I'm hearing somethin' too, but thought maybe it was just me." Tad, one of the hands on watch and the closest to Kyle said. He looked at Kyle, "Did it sound like a soft, deep rumbling? Almost like an odd kinda growl?"

"Yeah! That's exactly what it sounds like. It sounded real, but it didn't."

Tad nodded and looked at both Beau and Rowdy. "That's exactly what it sounded like. I've never heard anythin' quite like it."

Beau and Rowdy looked at each other. They read each other's thoughts. Beau raised his voice, "Ok fellas, let's finish this up and be on our way. Topper, do ya think the cow can make it back to the ranch or do we need to transport?"

Topper was a part time animal medic, and helped Nathan's wife, Robin, the ranch veterinarian, when he wasn't glued to his other duties or helping Genny with the level one riding classes. He was an former army ranger as well.

"She's weak from lack of food and water and nursing the calf. I'm afraid we'd lose 'em both if they had to walk."

"Ok. Let's get everythin' out of the wagon that we can carry on the pack horses and get them loaded." Beau gave instructions as he casually walked back to Kitt and vaulted into the saddle to increase his field of vision. He and Rowdy both moved closer to Kyle, which put them in between the cow and the area the growls had come from. As they loaded the cow and calf, Rowdy put his rifle down to lock the tail gate.

The horses began to fidget and stomp as they looked around wild eyed. "Heads up boys," Beau ordered. "Rowdy, is that wagon ready to role? If she wasn't a member of that experimental herd...."

"She did somethin' to the latch here when she kicked it. I'm gonna have to tie it, we gotta get outa here. Somethin's not right."

Beau nodded his agreement as he looked around intently and sniffed the air. Kyle was amazed when he looked around him at all the rangers and marines in western gear. Their manner had all changed. No longer was he surrounded by cowboys, but experienced military men, ready for battle.

Also growing more restless, the cow suddenly kicked the tail gate, hitting Rowdy in the chest and throwing him back and down, knocking the breath from him. The cow bawled and fought the lead rope holding her in the front of the wagon. Several horses screamed and reared as a huge black and brown shape shot out of the nearby thicket and launched itself on Rowdy.

"Rowdy!" Kyle screamed.

"What the hell is that?" Someone yelled.

"Shoot it!" Yelled another.

"Don't shoot, you'll hit the Lieutenant!" Came another.

Rowdy recovered from the kick only to see a huge head with two yellow eyes and a mouthful of long, white teeth looming over him, snarling and growling. It snapped at his face, bit at his chest and shoulder and fastened the dagger like teeth onto his arm when he jerked it up in front of his throat. The monstrous animal released his arm only long enough to get a better grip on his upper arm. When it began pulling him toward the bushes shaking and tugging Rowdy heard Beau yell, "Get behind it! Don't let it get away with him!"

Rowdy realized that he had to help himself, they couldn't risk taking a shot for fear of hitting him. He had to stay conscious, had to help them free himself, but when he tried to get the knife from his belt the wolf went for his throat again. In the back of his mind, he knew he was losing blood and would go into shock before long. He reached for the knife, but once again the wolf tried for his throat then sank its large canines into his arm.

"Stay back, Kyle!" Beau shouted trying to get a clear shot at the biggest wolf he'd ever seen. He couldn't risk a shot for fear of hitting Rowdy who was being drug toward the thicket. Several of the cowboys shot their rifles into the air hoping to frighten the animal away, but they had no effect. Rowdy was trying to protect his throat from the vicious teeth that bit and tore.

Finally, Beau's bullet hit the snarling beast, but had little effect. It didn't seem to slow it down or scare it off. Kyle dug into his pocket and pulled out his new Explosive Glow Ball gun. He loaded and aimed at the huge head and fired. The paint balls hit the wolf in one eye and exploded with the thick, glowing fluid spreading over the massive head.

The wolf yelped, jumped back and rubbed it's eyes while growling, snarling and refusing to leave its prey.

"Crack! Crack! Crack! Crack!" Round after round of the 45/70 calibers struck the huge mass of fur after it backed far enough away from Rowdy. Finally, it went down and became still.

"Nate, Nick keep your rifles trained on that thing just in case. I don't trust it to be dead."

Beau administered pressure to slow the bleeding as he and Tad checked the multiple injuries. "Butch, get the medical supplies out and ready an area to work on him. Kyle, bring some blankets. I need you to sit at his head an' talk to Rowdy....about anythin', just keep him talkin' and alert. You understand?"

Kyle nodded, "We need him to stay conscious so he won't go into shock, right? Drina had all three of us take a first aide course last summer. Keeping him warm with the blankets will help with that too."

Beau nodded his approval. "Good man." He turned to the marine helping him. "Tad, get Yancy on the walkie, give him our coordinates and tell him we need him and the copter here ten minutes ago."

Twenty minutes later, a pale and shaken Yancy was transporting his son via the ranch helicopter to a waiting trauma team at the hospital.

Robin, the ranch veterinarian was on her way to their location to transport the wolf to her the office for examination. Bobbie and Lillie were enrout to the hospital to wait with Yancy.

"You should be proud of the boy, Drina. He did what the rest of us couldn't for fear of hitting Rowdy. His quick thinkin' and steady aim could easily have saved Rowdy's life. He's a good kid." Beau said into his walkie.

"I know he is, I just...."

"You can't be there all the time and kids can't be protected from everythin'. He's proven to be clear thinkin', resourceful and courageous. Those are all characteristics to be proud of and encourage. Look, Drina I need to get everyone together so we can get back to the ranch. I'll let him know you're proud of him."

"Ok, Beau. Thanks."

CHAPTER TWELVE

Two weeks later-

**** Beau helped his best friend step from the chopper and smiled. "Good to have ya back, bro." He yelled over the sound of the blades. "Kyle has been askin' about ya every day since the attack. I wasn't sure how much longer we were goin' to be able to put him off visiting himself....the girls too. You got people fallin' all over themselves worryin' about you and wanting to help."

Both men turned, smiled and saluted Yancy, still sitting in the chopper. He smiled back, waved and mouthed, "See ya later," and waited for them to clear the beaters before taking the chopper back to the storage building.

Rowdy grinned and nodded as he placed his left hand over his bad arm protectively. His injured arm rested securely within a sturdy removable cast and sling. "That's what Pop said." He answered as they made their way to the jeep.

Beau started the engine and pulled onto the gravel road and sighed. "How's the arm?"

Rowdy chuckled, "It's fine. I've had worse. This is no where near to when I took all that shrapnel on that last mission. I think the infection was worse than all the teeth punctures and broken bones." He shook his head. "I think that thing must have eaten germs for snacks." He changed the subject. "I was gettin' worried about Pop though. I think he exhausted himself. Both he and Bobbi have been takin' turns stayin' with me. It got to the point that the doc ordered them to leave and get some rest. I....uh....made them promise to keep Trisha out of this. No one told her....did they?"

"Nope. Your baby sister is happily studying her little butt off in medical school." Beau grinned as he manouvred the jeep along the winding road. "I pulled rank and had Bobbi and your dad stay in a nearby hotel when they weren't at the hospital. Bobbi kept us updated on your condition and Pop would call and ask about the ranch. I told him to stay there and not worry, there was enough of us to keep things goin'. That man doesn't know the meanin' of stop. I didn't have a chance to tell Bobbi anything. She told me that she was takin' a leave of absence, course she says it's cause she's tired and burnt out." Beau chuckled and glanced at his friend. "Gonna be interestin'. I don't think either of you are gonna be able to ignore your feelin's much longer, bro."

"You make that sound like a threat. You warnin' me off?" Rowdy asked with a half smile.

"Heck no! I think it's about time. I've had fun watchin' you two prancin' around each other." Beau said enjoying the dusky coloring that crossed his friend's face and chuckled.

When they went by Yancy's home Rowdy looked quizzically at Beau. "Before you ask, I have direct orders to take you to the main house so mom can see how her third son is doin'. Drina was gonna take the girls, and Kyle over too, so be prepared. Kaylee has been worried sick about cha."

Rowdy chuckled, "Never thought havin' attention from a bunch of kids would feel so good." He said and laid his head back on the jeep seat. "Man, I'm tired. I don't know how anyone can rest in a hospital," he sighed contentedly and fell asleep.

Beau slowed the jeep and tried to make the journey as smooth as possible while adding paving the roadway to the, 'to do list' in his head. He'd never thought much about it before, but transporting an injured person to or from the copter pad could be a painful and possibly dangerous journey. An image flashed through his mind of him rushing a nine month pregnant Drina down this very road, wedding bands gleaming on their left hands. 'Whoa! Stop the boat! Where the heck did that come from.' Shocked at where his thoughts had gone, he rubbed a hand down his face. 'Man, I must be tired too'.

Kyle shot out of the house and had jumped down the steps before the jeep even came to a stop. Beau put his hand up to slow the boy's progress and put his finger to his lips and pointed to the sleeping man. Getting the message, Kyle walked quietly to stand beside Rowdy. "Is he gonna be ok?" He asked softly, looking at Rowdy's pale face.

"A little rest, TLC, some good food, and he'll be good as new, I promise. I bet mom has been cookin' all his favorites dishes, huh?"

Kyle nodded vigorously and grinned. "Her and Bobbi and Drina have been cooking all kinds of things in three different kitchens. I've never seen anybody cook so much and do so many things in the kitchen and in a wheelchair like Lillie does. Bobbi and Drina brought everything they fixed over about an hour ago. It's like Thanksgiving a month early. The house smells soooo good." He looked at Rowdy again, "I'm glad he's gonna be ok. That was the scariest thing I've ever seen." The boy said reliving the attack. "I've been having nightmares." He added sheepishly.

"Yeah, me too." Beau said leaning his arms on the jeep roof and bracing a boot on the doorway floor. He smiled at the disbelief on the boy's face. "That surprise you?"

Kyle nodded. *"But, you were an Army Ranger and did all kinds of dangerous things and rode some really big, mean bulls."*

"Yeah, and I still have some really big, mean nightmares about some of those things too. Because you're a grown man, with lots of experiences doesn't mean it doesn't bother you. Just the same, that was somethin' I can do without ever experiencin' again. Rowdy is the same. He and I went through some pretty tight spots in the Rangers. He always came through for me, and almost died the last time. We both still have terrible night terrors about that final mission." Beau explained.

"Me too, about the wolf!" Kyle agreed. "I...I really like Rowdy. He's one of the neatest grown up guys I've ever known. 'Cept you I mean." The boy said color sweeping up his neck.

Beau smiled, thinking how much he wished this boy was his. "Thank you son, I think the very same about you...an' I'm pretty sure Rowdy does too."

Rowdy stirred then and wiped his face, noticing Kyle for the first time and smiled. "Hey there, Cisco! Sure is good to see you. You ok?"

"Me?" The eleven year old scoffed, "You're the one that got chewed on!"

Rowdy laughed outright then and clapped his hand around the back of Kyle's head, rubbing the dark hair. "Don't remind me. But seriously, I owe ya my life, kiddo. Thanks."

"Awww!" Kyle said looking at the ground and kicking at the gravel driveway and as his face turned red. "I didn't do that much. I was scared to death."

"Didn't do much?" Now it was Beau's turn to scoff. "Kyle! Son, it was your quick thinkin' that forced that monster back far enough so we could pump him full of bullets. You made the difference, Kyle. You made it possible. This man is alive because of your quick, clear thinkin."

Rowdy swung out of the jeep. "How about helpin' me into the house, buddy. I'm still a little unsteady." Rowdy asked smiling at the courageous boy who had yet to comprehend that he had saved a life. He couldn't help but think, 'This kid's gonna make a heck of a good man.'

"Sure! You just lean on me." Kyle grew an inch as he straightened and pulled Rowdy's arm over his shoulder and wrapped his other arm around the man's waist. They walked slowly toward the house as everyone came out on the porch to welcome him. Kaylee wrapped her arms carefully around his waist and reached up to kiss his cheek, tears of joy streaming down her face.

"Hi, Rowdy. I'm so glad you're ok." She said smiling through tear filled eyes.

Kaylee back away and to his surprise, Ava moved up to do the same - on crutches. "Well look at you, Tadpole!" He said, grinning and kissed her forehead.

"I've been practicing! I wanted to hug you properly. Kaylee's been helping me. I missed you."

"I missed you too, Tadpole," and held her close for a minute. "I'm glad to be home. You two are a site for sore eyes. I'm real proud of ya, Ava. Real proud." He looked at Kaylee and winked, "You two, Chickadee. You did good."

Both girls grinned and hugged Beau next while Kyle helped Rowdy into the house and into Lillie's waiting arms. "Welcome home, son," she said as she held his face in her hands. "It's good to have you home."

"Thanks Lillie," he said kissing her cheek. "Somethin' smells good. After two weeks of hospital food I'm starvin' for your cookin'. When do we eat?" He asked grinning.

He bent and kissed Bobbi on the cheek as he went by. "Hey, Bobbi. Thanks for stickin' in there with me. I know I wasn't always nice."

"Uh, no you weren't. But you weren't feeling very good either. Besides, it gives me plenty of reason for revenge." She answered, grinning impishly.

"I have no doubt you'll think of plenty of ways to make me miserable."

"Count on it." She promised. When he finally broke eye contact there were several smirks in the room.

"Come on into the dining room." Lillie called. "Everything is set out and ready. The girls have been doing all the running and carrying and have been such a help. Doesn't the table look wonderful? Ava did it. We have so many thing to celebrate and be thankful for."

"Whose plate is that?" Kyle asked pointing to a large platter piled high with food and desserts.

"Oh that's for Yancy, he'll be here in a bit." While she spoke in a very matter of fact manner, Beau and Rowdy loved the blush that spread across her face.

Kaylee tugged on Rowdy's jeans and smiled. "I found a picture. Would you tell me who everyone is?"

The cowboy knelt down and nodded. "Sure, Chickadee. Let me see."

She handed him an old picture of three kids and their folks. He sighed and hugged her. "Thanks kiddo. I haven't seen this photo in years. This is a picture of my mom and dad, and these three kids...."

"Yeah?" She said eyes wide in fascination.

He chuckled, "The kids are myself, my twin brother, Brody, and our little sister, Patricia."

"Um, Beau. Could I talk with you privately for a minute?" Drina asked as everyone was going to their own homes for the night. Yancy and Kyle had just left with Rowdy. They would both be staying with Yancy for a couple of nights.

"Sure," he said. "Let's go into my office where it's quieter. "What's up?" He asked as he closed the door behind them. "Is anythin' wrong with your cabin?"

"Oh no! Everything has been wonderful. The kids and I have enjoyed every minute of our time here. It's helped us to become a family. Thank you for that."

He gave her a polite half bow, "It has purely been my pleasure, ma'am." He said with a smile that she felt all the way down to her toes.

Well," this was going to be harder than she thought. "Well, I was wondering...." she caught herself getting lost in his eyes. They were dark and beautiful. She shook herself and began again. "I was wondering what your bookings were like for the next couple of months."

'Well,' He thought. 'That sure came out of left field,' and had been about the last thing he expected. He was hoping she would stick it out for the full three months. Looks like she was going to cut it short. He had hoped....

"Actually, we don't have many cabins reserved for a while. Not really something we purposely did, it just worked out that way. I'm glad now, it'll give Rowdy more time to recoup without alota extra folks around and will give me more time to spend with Ava and get all my ducks in a row for her adoption. I think it will be good for Lillie too. Why?" He made himself look into her eyes.

She took a breath and said, "I was wondering if I....that is, if the kids and I...that is if we could extend our stay. My song writing is going better than it ever has before and the kids are doing so well. Especially Kaylee," she smiled and hugged herself. "She hasn't been so happy since before the plane crash. This place has been like a magic potion for her. She loves being with Ava and helping her with the exercises and walking. This place and knowing you...all of you has given her a confidence and self worth that is....priceless. She loves Nugget to death, and learning to conquer her fear of horses and riding has made a miraculous transformation in her. It's...it has all empowered her, she just she is so much happier and better off. "She thought she might be prattling so she looked away from the too handsome face and made herself stop.

Beau was quiet for a moment. "Are those the only reasons? The kids are doin' well and you're writin' songs?" When he took a step toward her she swallowed. Maybe...if he could keep them here longer, maybe...."

"Well, of....of course those are all good reasons." She said feeling flushed and warm and, 'Oh my, his eyes were gorgeous and his lashes were sooo long.' "Ah reasons, yes! Well those are good reasons and we all have time to ride together and it's been good for us to get to know one another on a much more personal level. And....and I can pay of course, that's no problem and they really seem to enjoy attending school with Ava and Kassi and....and I love getting to know you...that is we...we have enjoyed getting to know you...all of you here."

"Yes, we have loved getting to know you all too," he said softly, stepping even closer and placing one hand on the wall by her head and leaning down just a little closer.

"I for one...would like very much to have the time and opportunity to get to know you much better." He looked at her as their faces got closer...and closer.

"You...you would?"

"Yes ma'am, I would indeed."

"I...I" she swallowed "I would like that too." She answered breathlessly. She thought she had never seen such beautiful eyes as his. Then they closed as his lips covered hers.

"Ya know," he said moments later, sliding his lips along her cheek. "the kids can keep right on attending school along with Ava and the other ranch kids.

She didn't think she'd ever be able to see a western movie again without seeing this man as the main hero. 'How could she leave? How could she stay? She was...falling in love with him.'

"School? Um, yes, school....they have to go to school."

"Drina! Where are you?" Kaylee called.

Beau forced himself to take a breath as he lay his forehead against hers, then gently kissed her hair.

Drina shook herself. "Um, yes so can we?" She asked breathlessly, not daring to risk looking him in the eye again.

"Drina....can Ava stay with us tonight?"

She finally gave up and looked into this beautiful dark eyes. "May Ava stay the night with us?"

He worked hard to hide his absolute delight at her confusion. "Yes to both," he said softly.

"Both?" She asked. "Both what?"

'Oh this was too good!' He told himself. "Yes, Ava may spend the night with you and yes, you can extend your stay," he kissed her lightly, "as long," another soft, sweet kiss, "as you like." He kissed her again. She had died and gone to heaven.

"Drina!" She jumped and broke the kiss.

"Oh! So...um Ava can kiss....no, no Ava can stay with us and um, thank you we can kiss longer....uh, um no, no we can stay longer. Yes, yes that's it, that's it, we'll stay longer." She turned so quickly to get away that she almost walked into the wall. She hurried down the hall, "I'm coming! Yes, Ava has permission to stay. We'll need to pick up her things on the way over. Good night, Lillie, Yancy."

Beau grinned, hugged his arms and chuckled as he watched Drina get the girls out to her SUV. He turned at the sound of Yancy's boots and his mother's wheelchair coming through the door. Both had quizzical looks on their faces.

"Did you two have words, Beau? She seemed flustered." Lillie remarked.

"Oooh yes, we talked alright and it was a ve-ry pleasant, in-ter-esting conversation."

"Really?" She asked.

"Mmmm hmmm. She asked if she could extend their stay. I saw no reason why not so I said yes."

"And that flustered her like that? Hmmm. Strange...."

Yancy looked over her head at Beau his eyes dancing, and winked. 'Oh yes, things were going to get very interesting around here and he couldn't wait to get started.'

CHAPTER THIRTEEN

A week later -

**** Beau, Yancy, and Rowdy had made the decision to bring the herd down from the mountain pastures early and preparations were well under way. All weather predictions spoke of a hard, early winter. Adding to this, all ranchers continued to lose cattle of varying numbers to both wolves and rustlers.

Several videos had been caught with surveillance cameras showing the same scene. Huge wolves herding small numbers of cattle and taking orders from a couple of men on horseback. The horses wore coverings on their bodies, making identification impossible and their hooves were always covered so tracking attempts had proven fruitless. The thefts occurred during dry weather so no tire impressions were ever found even by the most experienced trackers.

While there had been no further attacks on humans, the size of the wolves captured on video and the prints found had everyone on edge. Sheriff Koni and her deputies were having no luck finding the culprits despite assistance from the State Police. All were taking considerable criticism because of it. Sheriff Keezheekoni, (Koni) Black Feather was the only daughter of retired Sheriff Hohnihohkaiyohos, (Hos) Black Feather and older sister of young Sheriff Deputy Avonaco, (Bear) Black Feather. Koni had worked her way through college as a Deputy for her father, had earned a Bachelors Degree in Law Enforcement and a minor in Criminal Law two years ago. Her father retired shortly there after following a severe heart attack, and she ran for the office after her younger brother, Avonoco decided he didn't want the added responsibility and liked being a part time deputy. When he wasn't home he was still working as a Reserve Army Ranger. He had been in the service for several years and liked feeling he made a difference in both uniforms.

No one really expected Koni to win the election against one of the other deputies. He had ten years experience and she was fresh out of college. However, he was cocky, arrogant and known for making cowboy and Indian cracks. He had promised to bring the Sheriff's office out of the dark ages, but voters feared he would bring about severe racial problems especially when he began making disparaging remarks against Koni. He had anticipated winning to the extent that he had called himself Sheriff several times. But, the voters spoke and the embarrassed deputy had resigned immediately and moved out of state to the county's relief.

Unlike Deputy Dogg, Koni, her father and brother were very well liked and respected in the Department, the courts, community and the Cheyenne tribe. Deputy Doggie as he was known in secret had made no bones about disliking having to take orders from an, "Injun," as he disrespectfully called Sheriff Hos.

It was important to get the cattle closer for the safety of animal and man alike. The loss of even a few head of cattle could be a blow to any ranch but the loss of a human life was totally unacceptable. The level of danger in the air was such that Beau had even considered refunding the remaining guest's fees and sending them home. This idea had been met with a considerable disagreement. They had come to take part in the entire ranching experience, good and bad. They respected Beau, Yancy and Rowdy and what they did too much to leave them in the lurch.

Beau was uncomfortable with the idea of Drina being part of the round up. He told himself that she was the only adult female guest left and he felt responsible for her safety. He spoke of this to Yancy and Rowdy and was promptly laughed out of the cabin.

"It's not safe anymore." Beau argued.

"The way things are, it's not safe for any of us, son." Yancy answered quietly, biting his cheek. "Why don't you just admit you care for the girl and get it over with?"

Beau scowled at the man he loved like a father. "You're just feelin' all lovey dovey cause you and Lillie have set a date." He said grumpily.

"Ah yes, the date." The older man said leaning back in his chair and grinning like the Cheshire cat. "Seriously, I'm not sure how you're gonna keep her from goin'. She 'pears to be a bit on the stubborn side."

Beau rubbed both hands down his face and shook his head. "I just don't have a good feelin' about her bein' on the drive with all the things goin' on. It's bad enough that the rest of us risk the weather, that's what we do, it goes with the territory. But now, this situation with rustlers and these wolves make my blood run cold. And I don't want anything else goin' wrong for you and mom."

"So what are you suggestin'? I've heard Drina say they are paid up for the rest of the year and she is gettin' more quality song writing done than ever before. She thinks being here is helpin' with that. You can't very well throw 'em out." Rowdy added. "And look at the difference in Ava. Kaylee and the adoption is the best therapy the kid could've had."

Yancy nodded, "Not to mention the change in Drina's kids. Little Kaylee has blossomed like a rose and Kyle is maturin' into a fine kid. No more practical jokes or whining. He's great to be around."

Rowdy straightened in his chair and leaned over the table and looked intently into Beau's eyes.

"Fess up bro, you are goggle eyed over the woman, more so than anyone you ever dated."

Beau took a deep breath. "I don't want to risk her gettin' hurt. I...I don't think I could handle it."

Both men understood what their friend hadn't said.

Rowdy clapped him on thw shoulder.

"Ok. Now, what else are ya not telling us, bro? How could this have anything to do with Lillie and Pop? There's somethin' else, spit it out and let's deal with it."

Beau sighed, looked sideways at Yancy and then at his watch. "I called Nate and Koni before I come on over. Nate should be here any minite, it may take Koni half an hour." He turned and went outside to the truck. Father and son looked at each other across the table in total confusion and a feeling of dread.

As Beau climbed the steps Nathan pulled up in his truck After going in together Beau closed the curtains, locked the door and placed a small lock box on the table. After sitting down, he opened the box and pulled out a suede bag, looked unhappily at Yancy and dumped the contents on the table.

The three cowboys stared first at the key chain then at Beau.

"Where?"

"What?" They all asked together.

"Kyle found this when he and I pulled that calf outa the ditch down in the south west section where we lost those half dozen cows. It was caught on a thorn bush. Caught real good too," he pointed to the keychain, "the clasp is plumb broke."

Yancy had gone pale, "What the heck is goin' on around here? He's....even if he were alive he wouldn't got his fancy boots dirty by goin' fifty yards off the beaten path."

Beau and Rowdy both nodded. "I know, Pop." Beau said, "Just when I think we've heard the last of him somethin' else shows up....Is there any way it's a different one?" He asked hopefully.

Rowdy picked up the one of a kind keychain with a pen and looked at it closely. "There's no way this is not his, it's too personalized." He looked at it more closely, got up and rummaged around in a drawer for a magnifying glass and returned to the table. "There's no sign of rust on the metal....there's no dust or water in here, pointing to the little containers....so it's not been there that long. Did he....?"

"Yeah," Beau nodded. "He had it when he left, I saw him messin' with it before he got on the plane, and those are keys to the house and the Yukon. So. The question is....how did it get out on the range when his plane was supposed to have gone down in the mountains a hundred miles from here?"

Nate took the keychain and looked at the saddle closely. "Have you shown this to Sheriff Koni yet?"

"No, but I called her right after we talked this mornin'. She and Bear were on a call but will come on out as soon as they can." Koni Black Feather, and Bear; were third generation law enforcement. They and their father and grandfather were respected members of the community and of the Cheyenne tribe. Her father, known as Hos had been Sheriff for thirty years until the heart attack forced him to retire.

Yancy looked sick. "God, we have to tell Lillie." The older man buried his face in his hands. "I thought we could finally...."

"I know, Pop; I can't tell ya how sorry I am to bring this out." Beau looked miserable.

"Let's not get ahead of ourselves here." Rowdy said. "Let's take this apart - piece by piece and see where it goes."

They went through a pot of coffee prior to the Sheriff's arrival and another three afterward. They talked long into the morning and thought they had mapped out a plan. The first step would be the hardest for all of them. Showing Lillie the keychain that she had designed for Rodney would be digging up the past all over again. He had held the keychain in his hand as he boarded the little plane five years ago. The keychain that had gone down with Rodney and three others in the little plane deep in the mountains, none of which had returned.

⁓⁓⁓

Lillie stared at the keychain on the table. She paled as she looked at the keys and custom made miniature saddle. He had liked keeping several folded hundred dollar bills in his pocket. He had announced that if she really loved him, she would always make such bills available to him because he deserved them. And she had been so blinded by the rose colored glasses and his glib tongue that she had given in to his every whim. She had designed the saddle with little saddlebags that he had kept two hundred bills in.

She looked at Beau not wanting to believe what it could mean. Then not being able to put it off any longer, she looked at Yancy - her heart in her eyes.

"Yancy....what are we....? Oh. Yancy."

"Let's not borrow trouble, Lil. There are several reasons why that could have turned up." He tried to assure her.

"I thought once I finally saw through his trickery that he couldn't hurt us anymore. But he just keeps coming at us, even when he's not here. I'm so sorry, I've been so unfair to you all this time, to Ava! Dear God what I've put that poor child through....because of him and my own blind stupidity."

Yancy sat down by her and took her hand. "That's over and done with, Lillie. We'll get through this, find out what's goin' on and set it right." Yancy tried to put his own fears aside to reassure her.

"Pop's right, mom. We'll find out what's goin' on." Beau glanced at the Sheriff, "We've been discussing this and have come up with several theories. Thing is, none of them are very pretty but...."

"Pretty or not," she raised her head and said briskly. "Let's put it all out on the table and get down to business."

Beau felt pride swell in his chest for the mother he thought no longer existed. She had seemed to disappear when Rodney had come onto the scene. This was the first sign of the old Lillie that had been absent for the better part of eighteen years. 'Maybe something good could come out of Rodney the Runt.' He thought.

CHAPTER FOURTEEN

**** The October weather was already colder than what Drina and the twins were used to. Drina had not planned on extended cold weather when she packed for the vacation and what they did have was not sufficient for the severe cold they had been told to expect. So, a day of shopping was required. Drina had gained permission to take Ava along and as Kyle did not want to be seen with a, "bunch of girls" they were making it a girl's day out with Bobbi driving the SUV.

"I've never had so much fun in my whole life," Ava smiled after taking a huge bite of pizza. "This has been great!"

"Me too!" Kaylee agreed.

"Me three," Bobbi and Drina both said at the same time causing them all to laugh. Neither of the younger girls had ever had the opportunity to spend a day out for shopping with the girls and had thoroughly enjoyed the experience. Beau had instructed Bobbi to get whatever she thought Ava might need and to plan on her being outside more. As she usually had to watch the ranch kids from the picture window, Ava was thrilled over the idea and looked forward to helping make a snowman.

Beau had taken an older walker with a seat and attached skis to the feet, that could be flipped up when not in use. This would allow Ava to be safely in the snow and on the ice and he was already planning a skating day along with hot chocolate, roasting hotdogs, polish sausages and marshmallows. The ranch had several ponds that were suitable and safe when frozen. Now, if they could just get the rustler/Rodney thing taken care of.

In order to get a larger number of styles to choose from the girl group drove three hours to the largest city. After a day of shopping, laughing and talking, the group was relaxing over mugs of hot chocolate, coffee, and pizza. Bobbi sighed and contentedly looked around the mall when she put her cup down with a thump, splashing hot coffee on her hand and the table, with no sign of pain.

Drina thought that in itself was odd, but became alarmed at the sudden pallor in Bobbi's face.

Drina gently dabbed at the spilled coffee with a napkin. "Bobbi? Is something wrong? Are....are you all right? You look like you've seen a ghost."

Bobbi looked down and back at a sporting goods store, her breathing becoming labored. Noting the direction of Bobbi's gaze, Drina looked as well. Just outside the store two men were arguing. One, older and distinguished looking, dressed in what the ranch kids called, "dude clothes." Expensive boots with embroidered cacti and desert scenes worn over brand new Wranglers, creased to a point. His jacket was fitted brown suede with the same embroidered desert scene on the front and back yokes. His shirt was red and blue plaid, cowboy cut with blue pearlized snaps. His hat was snow white with a brown suede leather hat band, a circle of silver dollars decorating the front.

The man he was arguing with was smallish in size but well built. He was a cocky, arrogant man who got right up into the bigger man's face and was making obviously violent gestures. The older man sneered at the young one as he roughly pushed him away. He looked around the mall quickly as if checking for witnesses. Drina saw that his eyes widened when he looked their way and rested on Bobbi. She was alarmed at the animocity she saw in his face. He glanced at Drina then and stepped quickly into the store. Drina thought both men looked familiar but wasn't sure why.

She was glad that neither Ava nor Kaylee had been aware that the man might have recognized Bobbi. She looked back at Bobbi and was taken back at the change, especially when she began gathering things together. She whispered hoarsly, "Drina there's no time to explain now but we have go, we have to go, we have to get the girls out of here and leave - Right now! Now....Right now!"

Noting the change in Bobbi's breathing and the absolute terror in her friend's face, she too began gathering shopping bags. When the girls objected, Bobbi knelt down and looked directly into Ava's eyes. "I can't explain right now, baby; but please just trust me. We have to leave - right now - we have to....ok Ava? Trust me, we need to leave now."

Ava looked from Bobbi to Drina and back to Bobbi. "Ok, Bobbi; does my walker need to be folded?"

Bobbi was amazed at the amount of trust and insight her sister displayed. "Yes, honey. If Drina will carry your walker and Kylie will help carry some of the bags I'll carry you."

"Sure, Bobbi. I'm strong, I can carry my stuff and Ava's." Kaylee offered sensing the seriousness of the situation.

"Thank you, Kaylee." Bobbi answered without looking at her.

Kaylee walked quickly beside Drina and asked, "Drina? What's wrong? Did Ava or I do something wrong?"

"No! Oh, baby no. I'm not totally sure, but I think Bobbi saw something or someone that really upset her. I don't understand what's going on either, but if it upsets Bobbi this much and she thinks we need to leave then we're going to, ok?"

"Ok." Drina smiled at the younger sister she loved so much and kissed her forehead. "That's my girl."

They had gotten far enough through the mall that the glass doors were in sight. Bobbi stopped and set down on a bench and put Ava down beside her. She was so pale and breathing so hard and fast that Ava became frightened.

"Drina! Drina, come back, somethings wrong!" Ava called softly but urgently. She placed her hand on Bobbi's arm.

"Bobbi? Are you all right? You look all white and you're shaking. Drina!"

Drina and Kaylee ran back to the bench and set their packages down. Drina knelt directly in front of Bobbi and took her hands.

"Bobbi. Honey, you have to talk to me. This is scaring the girls - scaring me too. What's going on? You're shaking like a leaf and your skin is getting clammy....I think you're going into shock. Maybe we should get a hotel room for the ni'..."

"No! No, we can't s-s-stay h-here. We have to leave. We have to go home. It isn't safe here...we're....we're not safe here," Bobbi said. Drina could tell that Bobbi was working hard to keep it together for the girl's sake, but it was taking its toll.

"Ok," Drina soothed and rubbed her hands up and down Bobbi's arms. "Then we need to call the ranch and let them know."

Bobbi nodded, nodded and nodded again before finally pulling her cell phone from her pocket and nearly dropped it.

"Take a breath, Bobbi," Drina urged, they need to be able to understand what you say."

Bobbi nodded, took a breath with her eyes closed and visualized him, her tower of strength. She took another breath and used one touch dialing to call him.

Drina and Kaylee began gathering the rest of the bags and Drina picked Ava up. "While you're doing that, we're going to run this stuff out to the truck. I'll get the girls settled and come back for you. Ok?"

"Ok...Ok...Ok." Bobbi said trying to take back control. Drina and the girls rushed to the truck just as Bobbi's call was answered.

"Talk to me, baby," Came a deep voice on the other end of the line.

Bobbi closed her eyes and took a deep steadying breath. Turning her head to ensure the others were far enough away and could not hear the conversation.

"S....s....some....th....thin' ha....ppened," she whispered in a shaky voice.

There was silence on the other end. "Bobbi? What's up, babe? Are you alright? What about the others? Are they ok?"

"They're all fine but....but I'm....I saw him. I saw th....the runt. I know I couldn't have....but I did." She ended almost in tears. "I'm so sc.... sca-a-ared."

The cowboy grabbed the walkie from his belt and called Beau. "Talk to me, baby. Tell me where you are and what you saw." When Beau answered his phone, Rowdy set the walkie on the table, enabling Beau to overhear the conversation.

She told him about seeing the two men and who they looked like. "Where are you, baby? Did Ava see them?"

"No, b....but I think Drina m....m....may have b....but she didn't know wh....who they were, j....just that I got up....s....set. I haven't told her, I....I couldn't tell her. She'd think I'm crazy....I think I'm crazy!"

"You're not crazy, honey; now where are you?"

She told him the name of the city and mall. "Rowdy. I'm not sure I can drive back." She began shaking harder. "I'm shaking so b....b....bad I had to put Ava down, I was afraid I'd drop her. Drina took everything and the g....g....girls to the truck and is comin' back for me....but she doesn't know the way back yet. Rowdy....I....."

Once Beau understood the situation he got Yancy on the walkie and sent him to the helo pad to ready the copter.

"It's ok, honey. We're on our way. We'll meet you at the crossroads just outside town there by the airport. Know where I'm talkin about?" He talked as he and Beau met at the jeep and went together to the helo shed. "Pop's goin' to fly us out and Beau will bring Drina and the girls back. Pop and I will bring you back with us. Ok? Understand?"

By this time Bobbi's teeth were chattering. "Ok, ok, ok," She said nodding jerkily as Drina came running back. "Drina's back."

"Ok. I need to you do somethin' for me."

"Ok...."

"Remember your breathing exercises. You're havin' a panic attack, honey. You need to get a handle on it and we'll be there as soon as we can. Now let me talk to Drina."

"Ok....ok....ok."

Drina smiled, "You ok, sweetie? I got the girls settled and locked in the Yukon. They're safe. Now breathe with me and get some control, ok?"

Bobbi nodded and began to take deep breaths through the nose and out the mouth and handed the phone to Drina. Rowdy explained about the meeting place and explained to her how to get to there.

"I think she's having a panic attack, Rowdy. You don't know how glad I am that you can meet us. I'm afraid she's going into shock." Drina told him.

Drina got Bobbi settled into the Yukon and steered the vehicle out of the parking lot. She took a moment at the traffic light to take a breath herself and closed her eyes. *"Ok Dear Lord, I need Your strength and Your guidance. Please help me get us safely to the designated meeting place and get Bobbi the help she needs. Please send the calming breath of life into her and we will forever Thank you. Amen."*

Thirty minutes later Drina pulled the Yukon over to the side of the road, turned onto the paved area and turned the vehicle off. It wasn't long before they heard a loud whum, whum, whum. A bright light lit the night sky, nearly blinding the vehicles occupants.

"Ooooh - cool!" Kaylee said as she watched the helo lights get closer and hover before decending straight down.

Drina covered her eyes as the bird landed a distance away in an empty lot. Two men jumped out, bent low and ran for the Yukon while holding onto their hats. She noticed that one of the men carried a military grade medical kit and the other carried an army green blanket under one arm.

Beau and Rowdy both smiled at the girls after opening the passenger door. "Fancy runnin' into you ladies on our nightly flight!" Beau said smiling at the two younger girls and winked at them.

Drina noted that the smile didn't quite reach his eyes and hoped the girls didn't notice.

Rowdy winked at Kaylee and Ava then as he opened the front passenger door, and took Bobbi's hands in his when she turned to him. He looked directly into her eyes, took the blanket from Beau and placed it around her shoulders. As an Army Ranger he had been the Team Medic and was one of the trained paramedics for the Ranch. He framed her face with his hands and smiled warmly as he checked her eyes, noting the irises did not react satisfactorily to his penlight and her skin was clammy.

"I need to look you over, honey. Alright?"

Bobbi nodded her understanding and squeezed his hands. She was still shaking and chilled. "I....I....swear....I saw him...."

"Let's get you out on the hood where the helo's light is better." He gently picked her up, holding her close before placing her on the warm hood.

Beau wrapped the blanket more tightly around her shaking shoulders and hopped up on the hood next to her so he could rub some warmth back into her. "We know, hon. You're not crazy, ok. We'll explain everythin' tomorrow." Beau rubbed her back soothingly as Rowdy went to work.

Rowdy checked her pulse, blood pressure, heart rate, and eyes. He nodded to Beau, "We're good to go, but we need to get her home pronto. She's definitely in shock, bro. I'll take her back with us, you drive Drina and the girls back!" Before Beau could nod Rowdy closed his medical kit, and lifted both it and Bobbi with ease and made for the bird.

Beau watched as the chopper took off with Rowdy and his sister in it. He then opened the driver's side door. "Mind scootin' over, ma'am?" He said with his best smile.

Drina smiled back, and did as he asked as the girls looked on. "Daddy, is everything alright, is Bobbi gonna be ok?" Ava sounded a bit worried. She was used to her father doing something along these lines, but only in an emergency.

He turned to face the girls after seating himself. "Everythin' will be alright, Tadpole. We just needed to get her home. She's havin' an anxiety attack. That's all. You've seen Gen have them before, remember? And since Drina is unfamiliar with the roads we just thought it might be better for me to drive y'all home. Beside, it's been a good, long time since I had three lovely ladies all to myself." He grinned a Drina, "Not to mention now, I get to play with this new rig a bit more."

Ava and Kaylee grinned and promptly went to sleep.

"Is it normal for Bobbi to have panic attacks?" Drina whispered low.

The cowboy behind the wheel shook his head and pulled the vehicle back onto the road and headed for home. "She used to when she was a kid, but not in a long time. She used to have plenty of them. You want to explain to me what happened? We have a long drive home."

Drina looked back at the girls and was glad they had dozed off and nodded. "When did the panic attacks start?"

Beau looked at her oddly and none too pleased that she didn't immediately answer his question. He thought for a minute. "I think she was about seven or eight. We had lost dad....he had been gone a couple years and mom had married Smithe. Why?"

"It might be to our benefit if we knew when and maybe why. I thought strongly about becoming a therapist for a while when I was getting my BSW. When a kid has panic attacks, it's always good if you can pinpoint when they first began and what was going on in the child's life."

It was after midnight when Beau finally pulled up in front of his own cabin. He felt like crap, had all day and most of the night before. Yancy was waiting in the mud room and jogged out to meet him.

"How is she, pop?" He asked as he unbuckled Drina, whom had fallen asleep not long after the girls.

"She's better. She's still a bit shaky, and is staying with Randy tonight. He refused to let her out of his sight."

Beau nodded, "Would you help me get the girls to Ava's room and I'll get Drina to the mine. I'll sleep in the study tonight."

The older man nodded and lifted Ava into his arms and headed inside. Beau took Kaylee in next and settled her into the other twin bed. He returned to the Yukon for Drina and lifted her into his strong arms. She was so tiny and weighed almost nothing. When she sighed and snuggled closer, he held her against his chest and drew her fragrance into his lungs. She seemed to fit as if she belonged there.

In his room he lay her on the bed and removed her coat and boots, then covered her. He watched her sleep for just a moment then went to his study and sat on the couch. All of a sudden he felt worse, his stomach rolled, and a sudden, massive headache hit.

Yancy handed him a cup of peppermint tea and sighed. "You're a bit pale, son."

"This is just gettin' worse, pop. Bobbi's reaction tonight has me even more worried. I have a very bad feelin' about this. She was showing signs of PTSD, now that I think about it Genny shows those signs as well. I think we need to have a talk with those two and soon."

The older man nodded. "I agree with your assessment, Beau. Might I also add that you're not lookin' so hot yourself. You've been workin' way too hard lately, and with this extra stress it can't be doin' you much good." He placed a hand on his boss's forehead and nodded. "Son, you have a fever. I suggest takin' a few days off and get some much needed rest. You're not Superman ya know. Let me get you somethin' to take the fever down and maybe help with the aches and pains that you don't want me to know about."

Beau chuckled and broke into a coughing fit. "I'll think about it." He rubbed his pounding head and lay on the couch.

Yancy nodded. "That's all I ask buuuut remember that if you have that bug that's goin' round.... you keep workin' and you're just goin' to spread it around ta others." Before Yancy turned the lights out, he covered Beau with warm blankets, placed the bottle of Tylenol on the table in easy reach along with the teapot and left.

CHAPTER FIFTEEN

Next morning -

**** Beau opened his eyes to find Drina sitting on the couch next to him. She smiled and held up a small glass of orange juice. His head pounded and his stomach churned. "Hey...." Was all he got out before he got sick into the bucket left beside him.

Drina winced and offered him a glass of water to rinse his mouth. That done, he lay back onto the pillow she'd placed beneath his head earlier.

"Hey. Yancy said you weren't feeling well, so I came over to check on you."

Beau groaned and tried to sit up. "Bobbi....?"

"She's fine. Though, I think you need to speak with her - when you're better. There's something....I don't know. She's wanting to talk about it, but she is afraid of something. That was no ordinary panic attack, Beau. She was terrified. She acted like someone was after her."

He nodded before throwing up again. He rinsed his mouth, cleared his throat and tried to get up. "I need to see to the horses."

"I don't think so, cowboy!" She said pressing him back onto the pillows. She couldn't help but notice how strong and hard his shoulders were. 'Get a grip,' she told herself. 'The man is sick.'

"You're staying home today. But, we do need to get you into bed. Rowdy is on his way to help with that. Yancy said he'll take care of the horses and everything else you do will be divided up between the others. I told them I would look after you while you're ill and keep you inside and that is what I'm going to do. Whether you like it or not!"

"I was an Army Ranger, damn it. I've fought in worse shape than this and come out on top!" He might have sounded bigger, meaner, more serious if he hasn't croaked like a frog.

"Well, Hero, I'm glad you were able to do that. But fortunately, this is not a war and you have the flu and there are enough people around who want to help so you can take it easy a few days. Go change your clothes, get into bed and stay there! If I have to tie you down, I will! If you fight the flu, not only do you lose, but you subject others to the germ. Rowdy will check when he comes over to see if there is anything else you want done. Oh, and thank you for the use of your bed last night. I must have really been tired. I don't remember coming in at all."

He groaned knowing full well that she was right and that Rowdy would love to help tie him down - and crow about it for months. "You win, and ya didn't walk in, you were asleep so I carried ya and you're welcome."

She stared at him open mouthed a minute. Then looked quickly away, cleared her throat and said, "Um, now. The girls are staying with Yancy until this blows over. I need to get your temp down, I know you've got a fever, but not sure just how high it is."

He nodded and slowly pushed himself into a sitting position. He waited for the room to stop spinning then smiled weakly at her. "You sound like a drill Sergeant. Like bossing me around, don't ya?"

Drina flicked the thermometer a few times and grinned. "Well, I figure it's only right. I mean you bossed me around first. So...." He laughed, but was cut off when he started coughing hard.

When he was able to breathe again she smiled. "I'm sorry, I know that hurts. Open up and hold this under your tongue."

That is how Rowdy found them. With a thermometer in his mouth and her hand on his forehead. "How ya feelin', boss?"

'Oh, now I'm the boss! I'll ring his neck later.'

Drina smiled and removed the thermometer and winced, "His temp's 102.5, Rowdy. Would you help him to his room while I sterilize this thing and get some soup started?"

"I can do that." He watched as she left the room, then he helped Beau up. "How do ya feel?"

"Don't ask. How's Bobbi, has she said anything more?"

"No, bro. She wants to wait and talk with the three of us and Drina together. It really rattled her bad. I was hopin' we were wrong about this, but when my girl says she saw him, I believe 'er."

Beau nodded as Rowdy helped him onto his bed which Drina already had warm from the electric blanket. "We need to have a talk with Gen also. She needs to be there. Today....we can't let this pass..... Don't give me that look. You can either bring pop and the girls here or I can go to them. But, we're gettin' this done."

Rowdy sighed, "I know it hurts, but use your head man. We don't want to spread these germs around. Ava's doin' so well, we can't risk her gettin' this stuff. You can be on the speaker phone and you have to promise me that you'll take it easy for a week or so. Alright? I had this stuff a few weeks past, remember? It sucks."

Beau nodded as he pulled on his green plaid flannel PJ pants and lay back under the covers. Rowdy placed a new bucket next to the head of the bed along with orange juice, a fresh glass of water the bottle of tylenol.

They were all shocked when they heard what both Bobbi and Genny had to say. Genny sobbed on Yancy's shoulder as he held her in a tight embrace. Bobbi leaned into Rowdy's arms and wiped away tears as he rubbed her back comfortingly.

Drina sat on the end of the king size bed. She had Beau propped up on several pillows. The speaker phone was in the middle of the bed between them. Her eyes filled with tears of anger and she could only guess at how Beau felt. His hand gripped hers, not just for her comfort, but his as well.

Beau sighed, angry with himself that he hadn't put the pieces together years ago. "Honey, I wish either of you had come to me for help. Any one of us would have beat him within an inch of his life."

Genny shoock her head. "I couldn't. If I had he would have hurt Ava, Kassi, or mama. He said he would and that he knew people that could make you and Brett disappear. I was so scared, Beau! Now Brett's gone." She sobbed hard into Yancy's shoulder and was ashamed of herself. Both for never telling her brothers the truth and for bawling all over Yancy. She and Bobbi both felt bad to dump this in Beau's lap when he was as sick as he was. He needed her help and all she could do was wail like a broken hearted coyote.

Beau looked to Drina for help and she nodded. "Genny, neither of you are responsible for this or Brett's disappearance. That's one of the tools pedophiles use to keep their dirty secrets, it's for their protection. You have nothing to be ashamed of. You were defenseless children, put the blame where it belongs - on his shoulders, not yours. We also have no proof that he had anything to do with your brother's death. Brett was on active duty. He would be the first to tell you, SEALs, Rangers, all Military men and women live with risks every day."

Beau started to nod but stopped when the pain split his head. "That's right, honey. He was only protecting himself, because he knew any one of the three of us would have ended him." They ended the conversation after Beau said he would be keeping the walkie beside him if he was needed.

"Thanks, Drina." he said getting drowsy in the warmth of the bed. "For everythin'."

Yancy just held the teenager, using reassuring words, rocking her back and forth.

Drina went into the kitchen and called Rowdy on her walkie. She explained that Beau had fallen asleep and she wanted to speak to the girls more.

"I'm so sorry that this happened to you two. People who do things like this are sick and evil. They recognize people and situations they can take advantage of and enjoy the power. He knew both of you would want to protect your family and would stay quiet. I imagine when he left it was when both of you started gaining some strength and were not as easy to manipulate."

That had not occurred to either of them. The sisters looked at each, thought back and realized Drina was right, that they had begun to balk at his attempts to get them alone. That small thing empowered them and gave them a little relief. Geniveve let her head fall onto Bobbi's shoulder and said, "Thank you. I'm so glad you came here."

"Me too." Bobbi echoed.

Before they left Genny asked for the walkie and called her older brother. "Beau....?"

"Yes." His voice was gravely and still feverish. He found his walkie and answered.

"Never mind....sorry I bothered you."

"It's ok, baby. Talk to me."

"S....sometimes," she sighed, "this is really sick....but I...."

"What is it, hon?" He asked.

"Well, sometimes he would howl...."

"Oh my God!" Bobbi sat up straight up. "Like a wolf....a wolf."

The sisters looked at each other wide eyed and pointed.

"With you too?" They said together.

"Oh my gosh, I had totally forgotten that." Bobbi said then, "Did he ever show you the claws?"

"Those big wolf claws? Yes, he'd slide them along my cheek and say...." Genny couldn't go any further.

"He said that if we made him mad he might let his big wolves have us for a snack...." Bobbi finished as they stared at each other.

Yancy and Rowdy were both just as sickened as Beau. "I knew the man was bad news, but this...." Yancy ran his hands through his hair. "How could anyone do that to a child? My God....how do we tell Lilli?"

Bobbi wiped the tears from her eyes and leaned even more into Rowdy's side. "Pop, please....don't tell mom. What that man did to us is wrong and we'll have to live with that for the rest of our lives, but mom could never survive knowin' the truth. It would devastate her. She would never recover. I do what I do, because of what that slime did to me. If I had known he did it to my little sister...." she broke down into heart breaking sobs and Rowdy pulled her into his tight embrace rubbing her back soothingly.

Beau was nearly sick all over again at the thought of what kind of monster Smithe really was.

Drina broke into the conversation. "Your mother has to know, Bobbi. You can't keep this from her. She needs to know and while yes, it will hurt her I think it will make her stronger after the initial shock wears off."

"She's right, sweetheart." Rowdy told Bobbi as he kissed her neck. "There is no way a secret this big can be kept, and since it looks like he's out there, she has to be warned."

Beau cleared his throat and settled down into the warmth of his bed and sipped on the soothing hot peppermint tea Drina brought him. "They're right, honey. Mom has to know. Now that he knows he's been seen, he's goin' to act....he has to. Rowdy....Pop? Are you thinkin' what I'm thinkin'?"

Rowdy looked at his dad and they both nodded. "Big wolves, cattle missin', the runt missin' and now we find his custom made key chain with keys to one of our vehicles and the main house?"

"Yeah." Beau started to nod then stopped when it hurt. "Yeah, I'm thinkin' that plane crash was a hoax, an' he's somehow behind the rustlin'."

"Yyyyuup!" Yancy agreed.

"Bobbi?" Drina asked tentatively, "There was another man there, a smallish man. I could have sworn I saw a badge on his shirt. Did you recognize him? I thought he looked familiar but couldn't place him."

There was quiet on the other end. "Bobbi?" Rowdy said softly. "Who was it, sweetheart?"

"It was Sam Dogg."

CHAPTER SIXTEEN

Thanksgiving Day -

**** The main house was, "Bustin' at the seams," according to Yancy. There were extra tables in the kitchen, dining and front rooms. All were laden down with enough delectable dishes to make the biggest, hungryest cowboy push back from the table and plead "No more!"

Lillie had been in her element mixing, chopping, cooking, baking and roasting. After her initial shock that not only was Rodney Smithe alive, but he was no doubt behind the rustling and had molested two of her four daughters.

Beau had talked with Yancy, Rowdy, Nate, Bear and Sheriff Koni at length prior to telling her. They had all their facts straight and laid the proof out carefully so Lillie could see they were being honest and straight foreward.

At first, she denied it was possible, then accepted the growing list of facts. But the hardest for her was what he had done to her children. What she had enabled him to do. She had been eaten up with shame and remorse. She felt she had hurt so many people, people that she loved, children that had depended on her for protection.

Drina had found her in the garden one afternoon, crying. "Lillie?" Drina asked quietly not knowing if she should invade her privacy. "Can I help?"

Lillie shook her head, "Nothing can help, there's too much damage. It's too late."

"No, no it's not too late." Drina said fervently.

"How would you know? Do you know what my children endured? They begged me to not make them go with Rodney. He said he wanted to bond with them and I let myself believe him," she sobbed.

"I am so sorry that happened. He hurt all of you, you included. I do realize what he did. I've come to know you and your family and I hope you can see that some good is coming out of this. I know that your daughters have become strong individuals. Realizing that they helped to set the events in motion that made him leave has been very empowering for them. The counseling that you take them to and take part in is helping them to heal and deal and cope better every day. I've seen how much you love and support them. The fact that you took responsibility and apologized helped them so much. Do you know how few parents do that? And look at what Bobbi has done with her life. She fights and speaks for children who can't fight and speak for themselves and she can do so from their point of view."

<hr />

Beau and Rowdy stood in the fire spit hut that was just off the kitchen, and grinned as they taught Kyle how to BBQ a steer. Kyle was putting his back into turning the spoke and laughing like a fool.

"This is way cool!" He cried and looked at all the various parts of the device. "Did you build this?" He asked Beau.

"No, son. My father and grandfather built the hut. This is how it was done in the old days. During the summer we hitch a goat to the treadmill. We put some feed at the end, the goat turns the meat by going after the feed. But in the cold months we give the goat a break and man it ourselves. Sometimes by hookin' it up to a riding mower. You can rest for a bit. It's pretty much finished now."

Kyle looked at the mouth watering meat. "Where's the other half?"

"Some of it is in the big freezer and some is in the smokehouse. We butcher one head per family each season here."

"Cool." Kyle said admiringly, "I like that the people who work for you eat as good as you guys. I know people in Drina's business that don't care whether their servants live good or not."

"Well....they're not our servants, Kyle. We're all partners here. A ranch this size couldn't be run without their help. Everyone is an important part...." Beau was trying to help Kyle understand.

Rowdy took over, "The ranch is like a huge wagon wheel, Kyle. Each one of us is a spoke. All together we make the wheel and the ranch work."

Kyle nodded, understanding what they were trying to impress on him.

Drina came up and hugged Beau from behind. He turned in her arms and draped one arm around her small shoulders, pulled her up against his side and kissed her forehead. Others looked on from the kitchen and smirked. 'It's about time!' Was the thought going through everyone's mind.

"Kyle is learning about the workings of a ranch, honey." Beau said smiling at the boy he had come to love as a son.

"Oh really?" She asked smiling at the three of them.

"Yeah!" The boy said enthusiastically. "Do you know that they don't treat the people that work here like servants? Most of the people we know don't treat folks that works for them very well at all, 'ceptin you."

"Well thank you, Kyle; that's a great compliment. I don't see the members of the band and set up crew as workers. They're all....part of the family, all part of the band. Each person is valuable and helps to make the shows run smoothly."

"Like the spokes of a wheel!" He finished, proud to understand and use the analogy correctly.

"That's right, Cisco!" Rowdy said pushing the boy's hat over his face. Suddenly, Kyle became serious and looked at his older sister. "What's the wheel doin' now with you not doin' concerts?"

"Well, some of them have taken a paid vacation, some decided they wanted to change jobs, mainly to get off the road. Like a couple of them are working on Ben's ranch full time now. A couple others went to work for other bands temporarily. They're all working, no one is going without, honey. I promise."

Beau couldn't help but think to himself. 'When is she going to want to put the wheel back on the wagon?' He knew it would kill him if/

when she went back on the road. He didn't know if he was up to it, if he could let them go - let her go. She was like the hub of his wheel now.... the center of everything to him. Some day he had to tell her - but was afraid it would be to no avail.

Drina too, was wondering about that. She loved performing, she had a responsibility to so many people. She knew she had to make a decision soon. Before their vacation had started a concert had been scheduled on Valentine's Day, three months away. The thought of leaving, of not being with Beau nearly brought her to her knees. But, what about all those people that depended on her. And the twins, they loved it here and both were asking to stay. How could she give up being with them every day? But, how could she make them leave? They loved everything about the ranch, riding the horses, working with the hands, the school. How could she take them away from all that?

Kyle looked down and scuffed his boot into the dirt. "Kyle? What's wrong son?" Beau asked quietly.

"It's just, everything would be perfect if Eli was here." He answered looking glum.

Just then, the big SUV came around the house and parked by the hut.

"Just what we need," Beau muttered keeping a straight face. "More mouths to feed."

The back door flew open and Eli jumped out, "Happy turkey day!" He shouted grinning as the boys ran toward each other. They grabbed each other's arms and danced and jumped around in a circle yelling and laughing together.

Drina kissed Beau's cheek and whispered, "Thank you," before leaving the warmth of his arms and ran toward Ben and Riley. They were all talking, laughing and hugging when Kaylee stepped out of the kitchen door and held it open. Ava came through on her crutches and walked to the railing of the deck and waited as Kaylee rang the dinner triangle.

Once they had everyone's attention Ava announced, "Nana says dinner is ready as soon as you guys get the meat cut and into the house."

The girls both bowed together and said, "Thank you!" In unison, huge smiles on their faces.

There was standing room only in the dining room. Family, friends and ranch hands met together to celebrate the day and each other.

Lillie put two fingers in her mouth and cut through all the talking and laughing with a shrill whistle. She smiled, "Thank you. I'd like to say a few things before we set down and enjoy this wonderful meal together." She took a deep breath and looked at Yancy, who winked.

"While we have had bad things happen this year, there are so many things to be thankful for. In the last few months my relationship with my children has improved and I have gained a legal grandchild in the process."

She looked at Ava and smiled, and with tears in her eyes she looked at Yancy and held out her hand which he took. "And as soon as some.... things have been taken care of; we are going to have a small, quiet wedding to which you are all invited. Now, if Yancy would give the blessing we can enjoy this meal and each other."

CHAPTER SEVENTEEN

**** The December weather was far more inhospitable than Drina had ever guessed possible. When Beau had told her that the first snow in October, (which was a foot deep) was just a light powdering, he wasn't joking. This was going to be her first Christmas here with Beau and his family and the twins were loving it. She stood looking out the window of the main house at the heavy snow fall and shivered at the thought of the men and horses working out in that weather.

Kyle and the girls were helping Bobbi and Lillie in the kitchen and Drina could hear them all laughing and giggling up a storm. She however was worried sick. Beau and the hands had gone out into that storm over an hour ago and they still weren't back yet. She hugged herself and tried to rub some warmth back into her arms. 'Just when had it happened?' When had Beau become her rock, her world. She couldn't believe she had fallen in love with him! She didn't think she would ever find someone she could love. She didn't think she was capable of it.

This was never supposed to happen. She had no doubt that he also loved the twins, they were crazy about him and she loved Ava like her own child. But she could never ask him to leave all this behind and she had worked so hard building her career. She wasn't even sure he felt the same for her. But what about Ava and Kaylee? They're hearts would break when it was time to separate. Kaylee was already asking if she could stay with Beau and Ava, and Kyle loved it here. Both had stated they did not want to go back to tutors and traveling from one concert to another. When she really thought about it, she wasn't looking forward to the hustle and bustle of being back on the road. The crush of the crowds, the rushing from one city to another, changing outfits, worrying about the wierdos. She was at a loss as to what to do.

"Lord, please grant me the wisdom to do what's right by them all and give me the strength to do what You decide. Please, let Beau be all right." She prayed.

The front door swung open and the men all piled in from the mud room. Each one had removed his heavy coat and boots so as not to track mud and melting snow into the house. Drina ran to Beau and threw her arms around his waist. He caught and held her tight and close. She was trembling all over.

"Well, that's one way to warm me up." He said jokingly into her soft hair.

Drina's entire body shook as she leaned into his powerful chest. The others left them alone and Beau swung her up into his arms, carried her into the study and kicked the door closed. Once alone, he sat down in his big office chair with her in his lap.

"What's wrong, honey?" he asked and he rocked her soothingly.

Drina shook her head, "I'm not sure, I can't explain it. I just have this overwhelming feeling something terrible is going to happen and soon. Beau....I'm afraid for you."

Beau rocked the chair and held her close. "When you have a feelin' somethin' isn't right, listen to it. That's usually your gut warnin' you, but often times it feels far worse than it ever really turns out to be." He kissed her temple and rested his chin on the top of her head. "I won't let anything happen to you, Drina. I promise."

She shook her head. "No Beau, I'm not worried about me....I just have this feeling something is going to happen to you, and soon."

"Nothing is goin' to happen to me, sweetheart. You're worrying too much, thinkin' too much. It's less than two weeks till Christmas Day. Let's enjoy it."

Less than a week before Christmas -

Beau sat in his office filling out the payroll and bonus checks. He leaned back in his seat and began rubbing his aching neck. Drina lay on the couch reading her favorite book, 'Cowboy Mine'. She saw the fatigue in his face and stood.

"Maybe you should take a break."

He sighed, "Now you sound like Kassandra. She was in here earlier. A fifteen year old ordered me to stop for a while."

Drina smiled and began massaging his neck and shoulders. "She loves you and worries about you. You're her hero, her big brother, she's used to seeing you strong and with endless energy. It's a little disconcerting to find your hero is a mortal man."

With a groan of pleasure he leaned back into her talented hands. "A mere mortal, huh?" He sighed and leaned into her hands more. "I'll give ya a dollar if you keep that up."

"Dollars won't cut it, cowboy. I charge kisses." She said with a smile.

Beau spun his seat around and hauled her into his lap. He had caught her by surprise causing her to squeal and laugh as she wrapped her arms around his neck.

"A kiss uh?" He smiled and pulled her closer.

She nodded seriously trying not to laugh. "Mmm hmm. Only kisses, so umm, you need to pay up."

His lips were about to meet hers when they heard booted feet pounding toward the office. The door slammed open and a young cowhand bounded into the room.

"Boss!" David was around nineteen years old and Native American, and was Beau's newest hire.

"Sorry to interrupt, boss, but we found the wire cut in the one of back pastures. There's cattle all over the place, some's missin' but we don't know how many yet."

Beau regretfully lifted Drina to her feet. "Any idea how many are missin', Dave?"

"Uh....well....uh no, sir; it's been....we weren't able to start countin' for a while." He said looking uncomfortable.

"Weren't able to start....what's the hold up, David?"

"Um....well, it was the wolves, sir. They Um....they stayed between us and the cattle and right then there was only two of us."

Beau could hardly believe what he was hearing. "Do you mean there were wolves that close and they challenged you."

"Yes, sir. They did. We were pretty surprised at first, and....hell...." he rubbed the back of his neck. "I was scared to death. Never seen a wolf that big. Let alone so many. Recon, they're from Wolf Mountain. Maybe some campers angered the Spirit of the mountain."

"Did they offer to attack? Is everyone all right?" He sighed at the kids logic, 'I doubt that.'

"Tad's horse threw him when the wolves showed up sudden like. Rowdy says his arm's broke, but other than that we're all ok. I think if we had pushed 'em they would have attacked. Yancy and Rowdy are gettin' things together so we can hunt 'em down soon as it gets light."

"When was this discovered."

"'Bout thirty minutes ago. Tad's walkie was broke when he fell on it and I guess my batteries were dead, or somethin' 'cause it's not workin'. I threw some rocks at the bunk house and got some of the guy's attention. I'm afraid I broke a window, sir. I'm sorry 'bout that, I'll pay for it."

The three moved toward the mud room for Beau's coat, and boots. "No ya won't. You did what was necessary to get help and you didn't leave your partner alone. Bein' a dependable partner is a lot more important than a window. You run on back and let Yancy and Rowdy know I'll be there in a minute and we'll make plans." He slapped the younger cowboy on the shoulder. "You did good, son."

The young man stood straighter, smiled, jumped on his horse and headed back to the corral.

"Beau...."

He turned and hugged Drina. "We'll get to the bottom of this, honey."

"I know you will, remember that feeling I had?...Just don't get hurt in the process of finding out, ok?"

He opened the door, turned back to her and looked into her eyes a minute before wrapping his hand around the back of her neck. He bent and kissed her softly. "I won't." With that he disappeared into the night.

CHAPTER EIGHTEEN

**** While Sheriff Koni and her deputies inspected the crime scene and the surrounding area, Beau saddled Kitt. He had packed his survival gear as well as, Kitt's weather blanket, and some feed as did the other men. He and Sheriff Koni had inspected the damage to the barbed wire fence and found it had indeed been cut and the cattle taken. While the Sheriff and deputies continued their careful investigation, he and the men would have to go after the strays or lose them to the elements. He hated not being in on the search for evidence, but ranch business had to come first. He and all the hands who had been Rangers, Marines, and SEALs were auxiliary deputies and could handle things that come up unexpectedly.

Before they left, Koni's brother and deputy, Bear (still a Ranger) let out a whoop of success. He had found the wire cutters with what looked like some blood and skin and a boot print. Finally! Possible evidence. It was immediately bagged and Bear was in the process of casting the print which was somewhat unusual and familiar to the deputy. It kept getting more convoluted.

Beau was double checking the saddle girth when Drina and Bobbi entered the stables. Bobbi was dressed much like the men and carried a survival kit. Drina carried a beautiful silk scarf that she had bought on their shopping trip.

"I'm comin' too." Bobbi crossed her arms and stood as tall as was physically possible.

Both Beau and Rowdy just stared at her open mouthed for along moment. It was Rowdy who found his voice first. "Like hell you are!"

Beau shook his head. "No, Bobbi. It's just not safe. We have no idea where the cattle are, or if the rustlers are still out there. These men know what they're doin'. No, way!"

Drina watched and tried hard not to let them see her laugh. She had come to know Bobbi well enough to know that she was going to get her way. The men didn't stand a chance, and she was going to enjoy the show.

"Look, big brother. I love you, but I'm not a little girl any more! I can take care of myself, I have a good eye for details and I'm good with a gun and the cattle! I'll be a help not a hindrance. I'm coming....Deal with it!"

Beau's face darkened as he took a menacing step forward and put his face inches from hers. "Little sister, you stick to what you know best and leave the dangerous work to the men...!"

Before he could say more one of the hands called out, "Boss, we need ya over here."

Beau grimaced, spun toward Rowdy and gave him a look of total frustration, "She's your woman....you deal with her!" And stalked away.

Drina's jaw dropped in shocked silence as she watched him move away. His shoulders were stiff in outrage. She hadn't seen Beau this angry before. She turned her attention back to Rowdy and Bobbi as the argument continued. Drina covered her mouth and worked hard not to laugh. Bobbi had Rowdy pinned against the fence and was poking him in the chest.

"I'm the third B! This ranch is as much mine as it is Beau and Brett's! That means those cattle are a third mine! Neither one of you has the legal right to make me stay here!"

Rowdy sighed, gritted his teeth and took a deep breath. "Baby, look. I know you're good on the trail, with the horses and the cattle. I also know you have a good eye for details, I know that. But we don't know what we're goin' to find, this could be a trap and we would all be lookin' to protect you first and someone could get hurt. How would you feel then?"

Her eyes hardened. "So is that all I am to you?! A little girl to look after!" She took a step closer. "Let's review! I hunt, I fish, I'm a crack shot with both bow and rifle! Earp is faster than any of your nags! Also I know this ranch like the back of my hand. You know I can handle myself out there! You also know I'll just follow you anyway."

Drina cleared her throat and both parties turned to look at her in unison. "Maybe, you should both take a step back and breath for a moment. There's enough stress right now and your raised voices are spooking the horses, and the rest of the men are watching. They're worried as it is. Your anger is just making things worse."

Bobbi turned and noticed that the hands were indeed watching them with concerned looks. She sighed and turned back to Rowdy. Her eyes met his with pleading.

Rowdy took her shoulders in his strong hands. "Look, honey. I know you what to go. Believe me I do, but with everythin' that has been happening and all that you've been through....what if somethin' triggers a flash back? What if they're out there, and he is one of them? What then....are you sure you could handle that?"

"Rowdy, look. I need to go. The Runt is out there. He has a major part in all of this...." she waved her hands around. "I want to help take him down....no....I need to have a part in this. You can't deny me that. I need to know that what he did to both me and Genny, he will never have the opportunity to do it to another child. Besides, he's hurt all of us. Not just this ranch, but some of the small ranches that were really hurt by the loss of cattle. You may need a lawyer there to keep both you and Beau off of him. So you can take me along or I can strike out on my own. It's up to you, Drina will go with me. Won't ya, Drina."

Drina's eyes widened and she looked like a deer caught in the headlights. "Uh....yeah....sure. I can run in and get ready now if you like."

Bobbi turned back to Rowdy "See...."

He raised his hands in submission. "Fine, but you stay with me." He groaned giving Drina a good frown and turned to get Bobbi's gelding Earp from his stall. "Beau's gonna kill me."

After he had disappeared into the stall Drina leaned against the wall and began laughing harder than she had in years. Suddenly the women heard "She's what?! I depended on you to handle her, not the other way around."

The next sound was Drina's laughter and several of the hands muffled chuckles.

CHAPTER NINETEEN

Eight hours later -

**** Beau looked up into the darkening sky as the snow came down a little harder. The wind picked up, causing the snow to swirl around his face making it hard to see.

"Looks like that storm is movin' in early." He said to the others over his walkie. "I'm goin' to keep searching for that brood cow. We can't afford to lose her. Y'all head back ta base and get the cattle, and horses settled."

He looked back up to the sky and mentally added, 'Rowdy....get my stubborn sister home.'

Nate shook his head, and called back over the radio. "That's not a good idea, Bossman! What if the weather gets worse? You could be trapped out here alone."

Beau reassured him, "One of the emergency cabins is less than a mile due East of here. I'll be fine. The cabin has a lean to, so Kitt, the cow and her calf will be out of the elements and safe."

Rowdy lifted the walkie to his lips as Bobbi looked at him worry in her eyes. "He knows what he's doin', Sherlock."

Nate responded to his callsign and nodded. "Affirmative, Bossman. Sherlock out."

Beau nodded and spoke into the walkie. "Rangers...."

All the former rangers grinned and answered his call with one of their own. "Lead the way!"

Beau grinned, "Bossman out."

The former-Marines and SEAL chuckled to themselves.

Bobbi looked at Rowdy with a lifted brow. "What....was that?"

Rowdy looked at her with a half smile. "That has gotten us all through hell and back and keeps us together."

"Uh huh." She answered.

The week prior to Christmas, Lillie always hosted a luncheon for the hand's wives, and children. They had compared notes and decided who would bring what to the ranch Christmas Eve supper. Bobbi normally baked enough cookies for an army, but since she was still out with the men, Drina had volunteered to be the chief cooki-nader.

She had baked cookies for the twins before but never of this magnitude. Dozens upon dozens of cookies. Cookies of every Christmas shape, size and color were on every flat surface in the kitchen. The twins and Ava had a ball icing and decorating Christmas trees, snowmen, reindeer, wreaths, stars, Santa's, packages, holly leaves, gingerbread men, and stockings.

Yancy and Kassandra were headed for Drina's cabin with some of Lillie's candy decorations for the cookies. Kassi was telling a funny joke just as Drina burst from the cabin yelling at the top of her lungs.

"Aaaaaaa! Fire, fire!" As she danced around and ran back and forth in the snow, eyes wide, black smoke pouring from the screen door.

Yancy and Kassi broke into a run to get to her. He removed his coat and threw it at her and headed into the house. Luckily, Kyle and the girls were at the main house making a snow man. It was Ava's first so they were very serious and meticulous with its appearance.

They all three stopped and looked up as one when Drina ran out of the cabin. As Yancy ran through the door he yelled, "Where's the fire extinguisher?"

"Fire....oh! Yes, fire extinguisher." Yancy's calm demeanor jerked her out of panic mode and jump started her brain. "I...i...it's by the stove on the wall. Why didn't I think of that?"

As Yancy put the oven fire out he suggested that Drina and Kassi begin opening windows to let the smoke out.

"Yancy, I am so sorry. I'll replace the stove and pay for any smoke damage."

"We were goin' over a list of the ranch kitchen appliances a few months ago. Lillie remembered that one of the stoves was probably due for replacement, but couldn't remember which cabin it was in. I think you found it." He said chuckling and coughing.

⸙

Beau worked his way along the wide crevice as he listened to the sound of a cow's painful bellowing. It wasn't long before he found her and dismounted. The area where she had fallen was at least ten feet deep. He tied his rope to the saddle horn and threw the rest down the crevice.

It was painstaking work to make his way to the bottom of the ravine. A large female cow lay on her side. He knelt beside her head and stoked her jaw.

"Easy, girl. Ya really landed yourself in a mess this time." Her eyes were wide with fear and pain. He began to examine her closely and sighed with resignation when he found her badly broken leg. There was nothing he could do for her and he knew it.

Beau shook his head as he pulled his pistol from it's holster. "Sorry, girl." The sound of the weapon's discharge echoed off the walls of the cavern. He sighed knowing that he couldn't leave the carcass, so he did what he had to so as the keep it from spoiling.

⸙

Back at the main house the residents all turned to look outside. "Was....that a shot?" Drina asked.

Yancy nodded. "The others have returned, so I would say Beau just found the cow."

"I don't understand." She looked at Lillie.

The older woman sighed. "He had to put her down, dear. That is the only reason he would fire his weapon, except in self defense, and in that case we would have heard more than one shot."

———✦———

He stood and cleaned his hands and began looking for the calf. A low bleating caught his attention. Hidden under a ledge was a young calf, to his shock, snuggled up against her side was a tiny wolf pup.

The pup whined and wimpered with fear as he knelt before them. She looked half starved and beyond terrified.

He lay flat and held his hand out to the pup. "Easy, litle one." Her eyes widened as she pushed herself closer to the calf and whimpered. Beau let her smell his hand then gently plucked her up. He could feel her ribs beneath that thickly matted fur. "Aren't you the little lady."

He smiled and slipped her into his heavy coat, then turned back to the calf. "Ok, baby. Let's get ya outta here." He worked her out of the little cave and carried her and the pup back to the rope. This would take some thinking.

Beau tied the rope around his waist and let out a singsong whistle. Kitt nodded his head with a nicker and began slowly backing up as commanded. As the stallion pulled, Beau worked his way slowly up the steep incline. He had to feel his way, and slipped twice.

The pup snuggled in closer to his warm chest and shivered. Her body was still cold and sent chills through his entire body.

CHAPTER TWENTY

**** Drina and Lillie looked out the large window of the main house. The storm had turned into an all out blizzard, and making things worse it was after ten o'clock, and Beau still hadn't radioed in. If he had made it to the emergency cabin he would have done so. It was standard operating procedure.

"Maybe, he made it to the cabin?" Drina said worriedly.

Lillie shook her head, "No, dear. If he had, he would have checked in as soon as he entered the building. That is a steadfast rule that Brett and Yancy made when the boys, Bobbi and Trisha were kids. Everyone abides by it because it saves manpower and stress, and lives." She rubbed her arms and shivered. "My boy is out there....in that." Tears filled her eyes as Yancy squeezed her shoulders.

"We'll be sending a search party out as soon as the storm passes. He'll be alright, Lil. He's a tough boy. Beau's a Ranger and he's his father's son."

She nodded and wiped her tears away as she prayed for her son's safe return. "I've already lost one son....I don't know if I could survive the loss of another."

Drina shook her head and made her way to the den. Beau kept a huge, detailed map of the ranch over his desk, she studied it every day. She had listened closely when Rowdy, Yancy and Lillie spoke of the lone cabin Beau would go to and ride out the storm. Drina thought she knew how to get to the cabin despite the weather.

She knew something was wrong or Beau would have called in by now unless he was unable to. She knew deep in her heart, in her very soul that Beau was in trouble and that she could find him. She knew because God had told her to go to him. She prayed for strength, guidance, wisdom and courage. After all, she was a singer, a song writer and performer. What if she misunderstood God's message? She could get them both killed. But no. She was sure The Lord would see them both through it.

She excused herself, went to and shut herself in the den. There was a huge map of the ranch on the wall behind the huge mahogany desk. The various areas of the map were shown with a number and letter designation. They kept it up to date regarding the location of the lone cabins, corrals how they were accessible and recognized landmarks. She had made note of Beau's last known location and that of the emergency cabin he would seek out for shelter from the storm.

Then she took a close up picture of the area with her cell phone. She was going after him. After praying for his safety she was sure the Lord was telling her to go to him.

She had entered the mud room just as Kassi passed by the door and noticed the songbird donning her coat and checking out a survival kit.

"Drina, what are you doing?" The teenager asked with a look of concern.

"Honey, I have to go find Beau. I can't sit here doing nothing. He's out there and I plan on finding him."

Kassi shook her head, ebony curls bouncing around her face. "You can't go out in that....you could end up lost or worse. That would make the situation worse than it already is. What about Kyle and Kaylee?"

Drina put on one of Beau's winter hats and turned to her. "I need you to tell no one what I'm doing, they would stop me. This is very important, Kassi. This is something I have to do. I'll have my walkie and cell phone with me and will check in with you once every hour if possible. Promise me."

Kassi shook her head, "Don't ask me to lie to my family, Drina."

"Not lie....just don't tell them I've left. Please Kassi, Promise...."

Sigh.... "I promise, be careful, Drina."

Drina hugged her and slipped out into the night and to her cabin for the remaining items she would need.

———— ✺ ————

Beau leaned over the calf as he rode Kitt North East. He had opened his heavy coat to share his body heat with both the calf and the pup. His hair, sweater and jeans were soaked clean through. Chills raked his body. He had developed a hard cough that sent pain through his entire torso.

The cowboy lifted his eyes and tried to get his bearings. He couldn't see his hand in front of his face, let alone make out land marks. Another gust of wind sent ice down his back. The pup whimpered as the calf bleated for her mother. Both of which broke his heart.

He coughed once more and grimaced at the pain that gripped his chest. He had to find the cabin, he and the animals were dead if he didn't.

———— ✺ ————

Drina was glad for once that the stable was empty of hands. She saddled and snatched Cricket, the mare that Beau had designated for her use as Odin was not trained like the ranch animals.

She had been out in the storm for nearly two hours and was freezing. Beau was out in this, possibly lost because of the severe conditions and possibly hurt. If he had found the cow and the calf was alive he would have tried to take it with him somehow. She knew he wouldn't have left them to make it easier on himself. She couldn't begin to imagine how cold and wet he was.

"Please Lord, help me to find him. Show me the way."

Just then, a puff of wind made the snow whirl into the air and Beau simply appeared out of the storm, hunched over....his saddle...why? Why was his coat open?

"Beau!" She yelled, giddy with relief but astounded that his coat was open. She made her way to him and realized his coat was wrapped around a calf and something else.

"Beau!"

He looked up at the sound of her voice and rasped, "What in thunder are you doing out here?" And began coughing.

She pulled an emergency blanket from her pocket and put it around him as she answered.

"I'm here to find you! We figured you were lost because you haven't checked in yet. My God! You're soaked to the skin, you must be freezing. I checked the map and I know where an emergency cabin is. Everyone is worried to death about you. Just hang on, we'll get there."

They both breathed a sigh of relief twenty minutes later when the lone cabin came into sight. Drina led them into the lean-to and helped Beau down and into the cabin. She started a fire for Beau then went out to the lean to and took care of the horses for the night.

When she got back in the cabin she found not only a calf but a wolf pup as well. Having been snuggled in the warm coat they were in much better shape than Beau. Prior to saddling the horse, Drina had packed a set of clean clothes and long johns for him. The fire was blazing and the little cabin was already heating up. She held a blanket to the fire and once warmed placed it over his shivering body and began warming another. She filled two buckets with snow and began heating water for coffee, food and milk replacer for the babies.

Thanks to Rowdy's experience in the medical field the medicine cabinet had everything she needed to care for him. He was burning up with fever and it hurt to hear him cough.

CHAPTER TWENTY-ONE

**** Drina sat next to the bed with the little heffer in her lap. The calf had already taken down one bottle and was working on her second. The pup had already taken two thirds of a bottle and was now curled up next to Beau on the bed.

Drina watched his breathing very closely. His fever had continued to climb since they entered the cabin about two hours ago. Though he fought, she kept a cool cloth on his forehead, attempting to get his temp down. She knew that she had to get the generator started soon. Genny had told her that every emergency cabin had a locator button inside, but for that to work the emergency power had to be on.

Before she could do that however, she wanted to make sure both Beau and the animals were well taken care of. She looked outside at the storm that only seemed to be getting worse.

"Lord, thank You for bringing us to safety. I ask You now....please help us to make it through this nightmare. Give me the strength and knowledge to help him in his hour of need. Give him the strength to fight this illness as it fights to take him from me. Amen."

As the heffer finished her second bottle the cowboy woke and began coughing once again. The sound sent dread sliding down her spine. His face was beet red when he was finally able to take a breath. Drina put the calf down and placed her hand over Beau's forehead. He was out of breath and he tried to rise so he could breath easier. She folded another blanket and placed it behind his head in an effort to ease his breathing.

"How's that, any better?" He nodded and she stroked his damp hair back and wiped the sweat from his face with the cool cloth. "Beau, can you hear me?"

He opened his eyes to meet hers. They were glazed with fever as he rasped out, "The....others....?"

"They all made it back safely. As soon as the storm eases, Rowdy and Yancy will set out with a search party. All you have to do is hang on till then."

Cough....cough.... "You.....should have....stayed put."

"Don't give me that, tough guy. You would have done the same."

He coughed, "....different..." he looked at her through half closed eyes.

Drina slid her hand through his thick damp hair. "No....no, it's not."

After he lost consciousness she pulled the cover to his chin, put more wood on the fire and threw on her heavy coat and his hat. She steeled herself for the bone biting cold. Wind and snow swirled around her and into the cabin as she fought to close the door. Making sure one end of the rope was still secured to the cabin, she tied the other end around her waist, grabbed a shovel and slowly worked her way through the thigh high snow. When she finally got to the shed she dug the snow from the door. Once inside, she studied the generator.

"Just great, Drina. You came all the way out here and you have no idea how to start the thing!" She lifted her flash light and was surprised by the size of the thing. The generator was smaller than she thought it would be. She studied it and found the pull cord.

"No problem. Just like starting a lawnmower." Drina began pulling hard on the cord. After three attemps the motor turned over, chugged a few times then purred like a kitten..

Kassi looked out the window and worried over the promise she had made to Drina. The storm had worsened, and if anything had happened to Drina it was her fault. The teenager shook her head.

"I'm sorry, Drina." With that she turned, ran for the den, and cried out. "Yancy, Rowdy!"

Both men ran from the room at the sound of fear in the girl's voice. "Kassi, what the he...?" Yancy called.

"Drina's gone!"

———————

Beau groaned as someone lifted his head and placed a steaming cup of broth to his lips. He tried to turn his face away, and was amazed by the strength of his nursemaid.

"Honey, you need to drink this."

Whoever she was her voice was soft and sweet. Like an angel's. It sounded as if from far away, yet he was sure he had heard it before. He did as she asked and grimaced as the swallowing action sent pain corsing through his throat.

"That's it. Small sips." When he had taken all he could, his angel lay him back down on the pillow. A cold wet nose touched his neck then a warm, wet tongue lapped at his cheek. The coldness of the pup's nose sent a shock wave through his entire body.

He forced his eyes to open a crack. The world was hazy and a sharp shaft of pain pierced his head. He groaned and tried to remember where he was and who was with him, but couldn't. Moments later darkness took him again.

Drina sighed with relief when he fell back to sleep. The more he slept the better his chances. Man, how she wished his fever would break. In another hour she could give him another dose of tylenol to help reduce it further but it seemed like it was lasting so long.

Having done all she could Drina was at loose ends. The horses were content, the pup, calf and man were sleeping. There was plenty of wood provided they didn't have to stay long. The cabin was well stocked with food, blankets and medical supplies.

She had given him a cool bath to cut the fever's hold three times now. It might come down for a while but would go back up. He was becoming more and more restless with fever dreams. He rambled about

Iran and needing more fire power. He called for a medic and ordered someone to guard the prisoner.

He called his dad and begged him not to leave. He promised to be good if only his dad would stay.

He told his group of Rangers to stay close, quiet and alert, the enemy was waiting and watching.

She hadn't yet found the call in button so no one knew where they were. She was tired, so tired and decided that maybe a nap would help. She stoked the fire, put more snow in the pot for water and checked on Beau. His temp might be down a little, "Thank You, Lord."

She lay down on the other bunk and was quickly asleep. She saw the cabin, but it was hazy and someone was at the door. Then there he was.

CHAPTER TWENTY-TWO

**** The man entered the cabin, arms full of dry wood. 'Dry wood?' She thought to herself. 'Where did he get dry wood? It doesn't even have snow on it.' He turned and closed the door easily, then placed the wood by the fireplace.

"Howdy, ma'am, my boy," he said looking at Beau lovingly, "has told me all about you. He doesn't know it yet, but he loves you like nobody's business. Me and his mom was beginnin' to fear he'd never find that, 'special someone'."

"Oh my God!" She shot into a sitting position. "You're Beau's father?" Beau looked just like him. Same cobalt blue eyes, dark hair, and the same heart stopping smile, though this man had a full handle bar mustache. She felt panic course through her. "Oh no, please....you're not here to take him, are you?" She asked, tears filling her eyes.

"That's not up to me, little lady. That's up to him." He answered, sitting on the bunk beside his son and soothed the damp hair from his forehead. "He's grown into a fine young man. I couldn't be more proud."

He turned then and looked directly at Drina. "I've been watchin' you and Beau, you make a right smart lookin' couple." He smiled warmly. "I was sent here to help ya out. The Big Man upstairs heard ya ask for help findin' the emergency button and allowed me to come to ya for a spell."

"What do you mean by the Big Man, are you referring to God?"

He just smiled at her. "You'll find that button by the medicine cabinet. There's a mirror coverin' it. That's in case some saddle bum breaks in. There is actually a code that lets the main house know if you need help or not."

"What code?"

"Well, push it once and it will flash in a slow, steady beat. Push it three times and it will flash three times in a group of three. This alerts the night guard that it's a medical emergency."

Her eyes jumped to the mirror in question, and back to Brett. She tried to stand but was paralyzed.

"Don't you worry none, I'll get it." He said and did just that.

"Th....thank you." She stammered. "Why are you here?"

"Oh....I keep a watch on my family from time ta time. To tell ya the truth....that's my job. But, I got special permission to help you tonight. I have to admit it's been a mite hard watchin' and not bein' able to do anythin' sometimes though. Lately I've been under orders to stand back and let Beau, Lillie, and my little girl find their own way." He said a sad look in his blue eyes, "Sometimes it's been real hard." He added with a catch in his voice.

"I'm sure it has been. Some terrible things have happened, but.... but some good things have happened too....and are happening now! Have you seen Bobbi at work? She's a wonderful attorney and helps so many children. She's grown in the last few months, so much stronger and self confident."

He smiled, "Yes ma'am, I have and I'm right proud of her. I thank you for the part you've played in helpin' my family. I've been wonderin' when her and Randy were gonna admit their feelin's." He nodded and smiled again. "That Rowdy Randy, he's made a good man too. Course, he couldn't not be and have the daddy he's got."

"Yes," Drina agreed. "Rowdy and Yancy are both good men. I think a great deal of both of them and Lillie is a fine woman." She said.

A softness came over his face. "Ah my Little Lil." He took a deep breath and smiled. "She got a little lost for a while, but she's found her way. I'm glad her and Yancy are gonna make a pair of it. He'll be good to her. Her 'n Yancy will be ok. They'll help guide all these young ones through rough times as well as good times."

He gave her a quizzical look. "Have you figured out what you're gonna do? I know ya love my boy like I loved Lillie. I know you like yer singin' an all, but you have to be honest with yerself when you make your decision. You have to remember too, that yer decision effects more than just yourself. You can make the people you love happy or ya can make them miserable. Nobody can make that decision but you." He looked at his son again. "Beau has carried an awful lot on his shoulders for a long time. I'd hate to see him hurt."

He patted his son's shoulder and bent to whisper in his ear. "You hang tight, son. I'm always with you." He stood and turned back to Drina. "Well, I guess I need to be goin'. There are others I still need to talk to." He smiled down at his son. "It'll be a while before I can talk to Beau again. He comes to the ole apple tree back behind the house an' we talk. He may not see me, but he knows when I'm there. I expect you to do the same. You'll find my stone there right next to Brody's. Stop by an see us before ya leave. Brody sure would love ta meet ya. Sure was nice to meet yer acquaintance, little lady. I hope I see you around in the future. If ever you need help just ask The Big Man. He'll answer you. It may not be the way you expect, or in the time you want, but He will answer. Just give Him time."

The cowboy went to the door and though he opened it wide, no wind or snow blew in. Drina noticed that one lone Army Ranger in full Battle Dress stood guard outside. It was as if he was the one blocking the wind.

When he turned to face her, the breath caught in her chest. "Rowdy?!" Shocked she turned back to Brett.

"One more thing...." Brett looked into her eyes.

"Yes?"

"Inside the compartment are files they're gonna need. Don't tell them until the time is right."

"What compartment? And how will I know when the time is right?"

He grinned, "You'll know." The cowboy turned to leave.

"Before you go," she said.

He turned back to her, and raised an eyebrow - just like his son's, she noted.

"Beau and every one here misses Brett. Is he there with you?"

Brett Sr. smiled, tipped his hat and melted into the storm, the door closed firmly behind him as if of its own free will.

⁓✲⁓

The pup's howling and the calf's bawling woke Drina. She looked around in shock. 'It wasn't a dream.' She thought. The wood pile next to the fireplace had been restocked and the mirror was sitting against the wall on the floor. There, in the wall was a red button....blinking bright red in flashes of three. Someone had signaled the ranch.

"Thank you." She said aloud.

Both the pup and calf were making such a ruckus now she was surprised that Beau wasn't awakened by the noise. Before making some bottles of milk replacer, she checked on him. His fever was still rather high but it was lower, and it was time for another dose of tylenol.

After the calf was fed she lifted the pup into her arms and smiled as the little lady latched onto the nipple without a problem this time around. The pup seemed to whimper and growl as she took the milk down with renewed vigger.

"Easy, easy. You're a bit pushy this time. That's a good sign. It gives me hope....hey that's it....your name....Hope."

Now with a full belly Hope worked her way back under the covers and snuggled next to Beau.

⁓✲⁓

Rowdy sat in the den, next to the CB Radio waiting for some sign from Beau or Drina. So far nothing had come through save the usual static. He was just about to call it a night and let Nate take over the watch when a blinking light caught his eye.

On the wall a red light marked 'East Cabin #2' was flashing. Hope lept in his chest and he ran to the open door.

"Pop, Sherlock! You two better get in here!"

Yancy and Nate hurried into the room worried looks on their faces.

"What's wrong, son?" Yancy asked afraid of the answer.

Rowdy looked at them with joy in his eyes. "Wrong? Heck no! Does that mean what I think it does?"

Together they all looked at the blinking light. "That's from the South East Cabin!" Nate said excitedly. "One or both or them are safe."

Yancy's face was pale. "Look at the pattern. Three rapid blinks. That means some one's bad off." He gazed out the window. "One of them needs medical attention and badly."

Rowdy paled. "We know where they are now, but even in this weather we can't do anythin' yet. There's no way we could get that bird off the ground; and we can't head out by jeep. We'd never find our way in the blizzard. Nor can we risk the lives of our men or any horses."

The men debated what to do, but quieted as broken static began coming through the radio.

"....Drina....to base....please.....is anyone there? Over."

Rowdy grabbed up the walkie and spoke into the mouth piece. "Drina, it's Rowdy!"

"Thank....I thought... I'd....get....Rowdy!"

All three men grinned with relief, but that relief was short lived.

"Good to hear you too, honey." Rowdy said.

Yancy took the walkie and spoke firmly into the mike. "We're goin' to have a serious talk when you get back, young lady!"

"Yancy...." her voice shook to the point even the walkie picked it up. "....storm ends....helicopter....fast....sick....fever. I can't keep it down!"

The men's smiles faded and concern filled the room. "Say that again. You keep breaking up." Yancy looked at Rowdy.

"Beau is sick....coughing....high....I can't keep....I'm afraid.... pneumonia!"

Rowdy felt his blood run cold. He snatched the mike from his father and spoke.

"Drina....listen to me very carefully. This is what I need you to do...."

CHAPTER TWENTY-THREE

**** Three days had passed, and still the storm had not lifted. Drina passed back and forth rubbing her hands together. It was Christmas Eve and Beau was showing little improvement. Again, she was unable to get through to Rowdy for help.

Beau's health had taken a turn for the worse. He hadn't opened his eyes in two days and his fever was staying at a fairly steady 102. She gave him cool sponge baths daily which helped take the fever down a bit, but it didn't stay down. Rowdy had taken her through what to do and where to find the medic kit. The sound of Beau's breathing was either a loud wheezing or almost none existent. She could have sworn he had stopped breathing all together a few times.

"Drina...." a low rasp came from behind her and she spun to find cobalt blue eyes staring into hers.

Drina hurried to his side and took his hand in hers. "Beau, you have no idea how worried I've been."

He coughed and grimaced. "....radio...." He tried to wet his dry cracked lips.

"I've gotten through a few times. They know where we are and will be here with the chopper as soon at the storm lets up enough." Drina lifted a cup of water to his lips and he sipped.

"Drina...."

"Shhhh, save your strength."

He gave her a weak smile as his eyes closed, he caressed her cheek and then his hand fell to his chest. Drina could no longer hold back the tears. 'Was he giving up....NO! He couldn't give up! He was an Army Ranger and they never give up!' She kissed his burning lips.

"I love you, Beau. You can't give up, not now, not ever! Ava needs you, I need you! What about Bobbi, Lillie, Rowdy and the other's? They all need you! Do you hear me! You've never backed down from a fight in your entire life! Don't you dare start now!"

Drina climbed onto the bunk next to him, and rested her head on his right shoulder. She closed her eyes and prayed for strength; not just for herself, but for him as well. It was close to midnight when exhaustion finally claimed her.

A few hours later Drina made her way across the cabin to the wash basin. 'Creak....creak.' She'd forgotten about the loose floor board while caring for her patient. Drina washed her face and hands then on her return to the bed, she caught her sock covered foot on the edge of the board, causing her to trip.

"Ouch!"

Looking down, she realized that the wood board was slightly raised, so she bent to pull it up. Under the floorboard was a secret compartment and inside sat a large metal ammunitions box filled with thick, very dusty files in clear plastic. On top of the box was the initials 'B.A.B,' and written on the side was....'Major Brett A. Blanton U.S. Army Rangers.'

"Hmmm. What's this?" She looked around the hidden compartment, "This must be the compartment and files he was talking about, but what is so important about all this stuff?" Drina looked over at the sleeping man. "He must not know about all this." Being a little nosy, she lifted one file then seeing the words, 'FBI,' and above that writen in large red lettering, 'CLASSIFIED.' she returned it, then hearing Beau's groan she covered the compartment and never spoke of it to anyone.

Christmas morning -

The dawn light shone through the cabin window right into Drina's face. She groaned and blinked her eyes. For a moment she was disoriented. Then it hit her. 'The Sun!' Drina was on her feet and at the window in a flash. A beautiful sunrise painted the snow with golds, pinks, and reds, as it sparkled like pixie dust. Ice cycles sent rainbows bouncing off the cabin walls and even into the building itself. It was the most beautiful sight she'd ever seen. She looked at the fluffy clouds and blinked. It looked for all the world as if the clouds were in the shape of an angel, it's arms and wings outspread over the cabin and its occupants.

A small paw rubbed at her calf and she grinned down at Hope. The pup whimpered for her breakfast. The calf also let Drina know she too was hungry.

"Alright, alright. Just give me a minute." She made her way to Beau and checked his fever. Her hand shook and she slid onto the bed her head on his massive chest. His fever had broken some time during the night. "Thank You, God!" Was all she could say before tears of relief ran down her checks.

⚬⚬⚬

Back home, the Ranch was a whirlwind of activity. Everyone that was able was busy getting the chopper ready for flight, loading blankets, IV fluids, food, water, and kennels for the animals. Nate and his wife Robin, (the area veterinarian) were taking the plow and trailer for the horses. It was stocked with fresh hay and water. As well as dry blankets and extra feed to restock both the lean to and the cabin.

Lillie and Bobbi helped two of the former Rangers turn Beau's bed room into a hospital room. They felt that was their safest bet for they all knew he would refuse to go anywhere but home. (Rowdy would be staying there till he felt his best friend was strong enough to no longer need special care.) As soon as he knew about Beau's condition, Rowdy contacted his doctor, who told Rowdy what, and how to proceed, and he would come out as soon as he could. Luckily, the ex-Rangers qualified as nurses and the ranch boasted a nurse among the wives and several certified nurses aides as well.

Rowdy double and triple checked to make sure he had all the necessary gear and grabbed up the walkie.

"Base to, Drina….base to Drina….come in Drina, over."

An excited voice chirped on the other end. "Rowdy! Oh Thank God, Rowdy, it broke!"

"What broke….the storm?"

"No! Well, yes of course, but I meant his fever….it's down to 99.9 and holding! It broke some time during the night! His breathing is still weak, and he's still coughing but much better!"

Rowdy sat down in relief. "Thank, God." He whispered below his breath. "Look Drina, we're almost ready to take off. If he is coherent make sure he knows and be ready for pick up ASAP when we get there."

"I will. Rowdy, the pup needs to stay with Beau. Hope has bonded pretty strongly to him and it would really cause problems if you try and take him from her."

"I hear ya. I'll do my best, but I can't promise anythin'. Just be ready. Nate and Robin set out with the ranch plow over an hour ago so they should be arriving soon. Like I said, they're comin' in the grader and the trailer for the horses and cow."

"Oh. I'm sorry, Rowdy, Beau had to put the cow down. Her leg was badly broken and he thought some of her ribs were crushed and that she was bleeding internally. I've had the calf and pup both on the bottle with the milk replacer. But I'm afraid it's nearly gone. I'll have some ready for her so she won't miss a feeding….what?…Beau says you need to stop yappin' and get movin'."

Rowdy grinned at the giggle Drina let out. "We'll bring some milk replacer to replenish the supply as well as the food stock….On my way. Over and out."

* * *

Beau lay in his room, IV fluids steadily dripping into his arm. Drina lay asleep on the love seat and Ava sat on his bed with Kaylee and Kyle.

Hope lay cuddled up to his side, her head resting firmly on his thigh while he stroked her thick fur. No one was sure what color she really was just yet, it was hard to get her away from him. Her fur was still muddy and thickly matted.

The group had moved the Christmas tree into the corner and the lights were flashing. It was a wonderful site and added to the relief of being home.

He felt like he'd been run over by a herd of mustangs, and was almost positive that's exactly what had happened. There wasn't a single place on his body that didn't ache. Even his hair hurt. Sleep was beginning to pull him under as his and Drina's gifts were brought in by Bobbi, Rowdy, and Yancy.

Lil stroked her boy's hair back and sighed. "Welcome home, baby." She kissed his hand and wheeled herself to the kitchen to start some homemade chicken noodle soup.

Rowdy grinned, "Spsst, kids. Let's get outta here and let them sleep. Beau needs rest in order to get better, and Drina needs it just as badly, she is plumb worn out from takin' care of the three of 'em. She hasn't had much rest in the past few days."

Kyle and the girls reluctantly left the room. Watching the kids, Bobbi giggled and pressed a kiss to her now sleeping brother's cheek before she followed. Rowdy checked Beau's vitals and nodded to his father. Yancy covered Drina with a blanket before both he and Rowdy left, closing the door behind them.

CHAPTER TWENTY-FOUR

**** Yancy stood in the den with Rowdy, Bobbi, Genny and Robin. "I'm not sayin' that we put it down, Robi. Just that this is no place for a wolf." Yancy slid his hand down his face. "When Drina said pup I thought she meant a dog. It never occured to me that Beau saved a wolf pup."

Robin shook her head, "That pup has formed a deep bond with both Beau and Drina. Sending her to a zoo or even an animal park," she shook her head…. "I have little faith that she would survive the move, and have you forgotten who else this plan would affect?"

Geniveve nodded in agreement. "I doubt my brother will part with her. She's slept with him every night." Gen smiled. "I really don't think she's that bad. Yes, she's a wild animal, but I've been doing some research on wolves, and what I've found out so far is that they're not the blood thirsty killers people think they are."

"Koni seems to agree that we should keep the animal, for now at least." Rowdy agreed. "Since wolves are being used to take the cattle, she thinks we might be able to learn somethin' about them that might help us."

Yancy looked at them all like they had grown beaks. "Do you people hear yourselves? Might I remind you that we have lost almost thirty head to that crazy wolf pack and one of them attacked Rowdy! If they're not killin' machines what are they?!"

Bobbi sighed, "Most of the information I'm finding is that they're very sociable, caring animals, Yancy. They tend to form deep rooted bonds and they will fight and kill anything that threatens their pack. They're very protective about their pack, their family….and Beau is her pack, her alpha. That doesn't mean I agree with my sister." She looked at Genny. "In fact, it is the complete opposite, but this isn't up to us."

⸻ ⅏ ⸻

Beau sat up slowly, glared at Yancy and placed his bowl on the bed side table. He was still very weak, his voice still raspy, and his throat and chest sore as he spoke.

"The answer is no. Hope stays with me, and that is the end of this discussion!" He stroked the pup's ear as she lifted her head and tilted it from side to side as she studied Yancy with her large brown puppy eyes.

"Because of her we still have a Belted Galloway heffer. Those two saved each other by sharin' their body warmth. I don't know how she come to be out there by herself, but....one thing I've learned through all this is that things happen for a reason. I believe Hope was there to help the calf survive. I believe I was meant to find her and she was meant to survive the trip to the cabin. I know there is a bigger plan and we're all part of it. I don't know what it all means, but one thing I'm sure of is that Hope is supposed to be here with me. End of discussion."

Beau seldom spoke like a boss to Yancy, Rowdy or Nate. He had virtually never used that tone with Yancy, telling them all how deeply he felt about the pup.

Yancy nodded his head and looked at Beau steadily. "All right, son. If you feel that strongly about her, I'll drop it for now. But....if we start loosin' calves, chickens, ducks or God forgive your mother's prized turkey later I can't promise how some of the others....your mother in particular will feel."

"We won't lose anythin' because of Hope, let alone any of mom's prized poultry, at least not after I've trained her. Besides, she'll be good protection for the kids, Yancy, you'll see."

⸻ ⅏ ⸻

Drina stepped over to the bed and stroked Hope from head to tail over and over. She knelt by the bed next to Beau and the pup. "You hear that, Hope? You're gonna stay here as long as you want and you'll never have to be cold and hungry again." She chuckled as the small wet tongue licked her cheek.

Beau placed his hand in her hair, moved over on the mattress and patted the area next to his waist. She sat next to him and lowered her head to his chest and sighed as he hugged her and placed a kiss in her hair.

"I love the way your hair smells, the way you smell. Have I thanked you yet for savin' my life....for savin' our lives? We would have died in that blizzard if not for you. I owe you in so many ways."

She sat up, smiled and kissed him. "You don't owe me anything, it was just payback for all that you've done for me....all that you've given back to me. I'm just glad it all turned out well."

"How did you know where we were?" He looked at the delicate hand he held before kissing it and holding it to his cheek. "You could have gotten lost so easily yet you set out all by yourself. When I get my strength back I'm goin' to turn you over my knee for that."

She frowned, "Hmm, yes I see how grateful you are. Actually, I knew where you were, because God told me. He showed me where you were and how to get to the cabin. Rowdy had said where Nate left you and what cabin you would be headed to." She moved closer and leaned in to lay her head on his shoulder.

"I looked at the map in your den and took a picture of it with my phone. I was looking at the East cabin #1 that he said you'd go to.... but something kept telling me it wasn't right. Then a light from the Christmas tree shone directly on the Southeast cabin #2 and then it moved down to the stable. And that's the path I took. It led me directly to you. He led me to you and then to the cabin. It was the most amazing thing. You are on this earth for a reason Beau. God has blessed you and you are part of a bigger plan that He has in mind for you. I don't know what all He has planned for you, but He isn't done."

"Well, I don't know about all that, but I do believe that I was meant to find those animals, and that you were meant to be here....on this ranch to save us. I believe you have a place on the 3B with us...." his voice became raspy, "I want you to think about it. About staying here on the ranch. I know your music is important to you and I'm good with that. But think about making your life...yours and the kids here on the ranch...." He swallowed, caressed her face. "I thought God had no place in my life anymore, but you've shown me that He's just been waiting. You brought me back to Him and I thank you for that. I thank Him for you. You and the kids... all three of them are all the Christmas gift, I could ever ask for."

"I'm glad, Beau. The twins and I love it here. They have been begging me to let them stay here year round. We all feel at home here, like we belong." She said and while she firmly believed what she said, she couldn't help but notice that he hadn't said he loved her. So....in what position did he want her to stay? Just as an extra family on the ranch? Surely he wasn't asking her to live with him. She knew that couples just lived together all the time, but she couldn't.

"You're so tired, it's all you can do to keep your eyes open. Go to sleep, honey; lay down here next to me and we'll open our gifts and have Christmas dinner when you wake up." He framed her wonderful face with his hands and kissed her gently, lovingly. She couldn't tell him she was in love with him when she wasn't sure if he felt the same. She'd talk to him about the idea she'd been looking into.

CHAPTER TWENTY-FIVE

**** Drina closed her lap top. She had just finished the application for online schooling, paid the tuition and book fees and pressed....send. She had decided to go back to school for her Masters Degree in Social Work. She could do the school work anywhere as long as she had her laptop. She wanted to stay here - on the ranch, with him. She had been doing some research online and had found a few places that she could study and be certified in Equine therapy.

While she knew Beau was very attracted to her and wanted her on the ranch, he hadn't said he loved her or that he wanted a lifetime with her. She loved him, so very much but it was important to her to set a good example for her brother and sister. She didn't think she could stay as they were. The kids loved being there and all the people on it and had blossomed and flourished here. She would fulfill the contracts for concerts that had already been scheduled, but she didn't want to tour anymore. She wanted to write more than sing songs.

She wanted to provide therapy to people suffering from trauma and to utilize equine therapy to help achieve progress for her clients, particularly when a disability or PTSD was involved. Riley, on the other hand loved touring and singing but worried about the long term effects on Eli, as she herself had for the twins. They had talked about it many times and at length, particular when they were together over the holidays. They were going to make the announcement at the Valentine's Day concert. She would partially retire and Riley would step into her place as lead singer for the band and Riley's son Eli, would stay with her and the twins. The question was....would they live here or find another place...off the ranch?

Beau stood out on the deck, mug of steaming hot chocolate in hand. It was early February, and his heart felt heavy. He sighed and smiled at the large pup that ran and played in the snow with the kids. Hope seemed to have a huge grin on her canine face as the kids packed snowballs and threw them into the air for her to go after.

The cowboy chuckled, then turned toward Drina's cabin, his mood soured at the sight. Inside, he knew Drina was packing for the Valentines Day concert. She had reminded him of the commitment the night before and asked if the kids could stay at the ranch with him.

"I just think, especially with them in school, they would be better off here with you."

"Drina, are you sure about this? They're your family."

Drina smiled sadly, "If I take them with me, they'll have to study with a tutor again and they would fight it. Then they'd just fall back into their old habits, and that sadness that almost ruined them."

He shook his head as if to rid himself of the memory. 'She didn't ask if she could stay, she didn't even say she wanted to - she didn't say she loved me either.'

Drina pulled out of Yancy's tight embrace and smiled. "Yancy, thank you for everything."

The older man smiled, "No problem, Little Miss. If you ever need...."

"I won't hesitate to call you - you, you're sooo much like my dad. You....fill that void." Drina smiled and turned to Lillie and her daughters.

Genny and Kassi both stepped into her outstretched arms and returned her hug. "I'm gonna miss you girls."

They chattered over one another as they returned her hug and stepped back. Drina smiled at both Rowdy and Bobbi and hugged them tight. She placed a kiss on Rowdy's cheek.

"Call me if you need a shoulder to cry, or complain on, or a big brother to beat somebody up ok?"

She laughed and hugged him again. "That's a promise."

She hugged Bobbi and they whispered support and plan reminders.

She hugged Lillie next and held her a long time. "I am so proud of you, Lil. I can see where Beau and Bobbi got a lot of their strength.... you'll keep an eye on him for me, won't you?"

Lillie held Drina's face in her hands lovingly, "I will, honey. You're sure this is how you want to handle the situation? You know he loves you, honey."

"I know he likes me, alot - but really doesn't even want to do that."

Lillie just gave her a small smile. Drina turned to Ava and lifted her into a big hug. The little girl giggled a bit when the songbird placed a flower in the child's hair. "Look after your dad for me, ok?"

Ava nodded, "Ok."

Drina had already said her farewells to Kaylee and Kyle. She looked around to see if he had come to say goodbye, but....he wasn't there. She was about to step into the SUV when a loud whinny caught her attention. She turned and found Kitt and Beau cantering up. He stopped only feet from her, his face void of emotion. His eyes seemed almost hollow, but he held his hand out to her and waited.

Drina swallowed hard, 'All he wants from me is a handshake?' She asked herself, but took his hand and gasped as she was lifted into the saddle. Kitt reared, spun on his back legs and took off like a bullet. Drina wrapped her arms around the cowboy's waist for dear life, until they stopped almost a mile from the house.

"Drina,...."

She looked up into his cobalt blue eyes. "Beau...."

"You were really goin' to leave without sayin' goodbye?"

There was no emotion in his voice at all and that hurt. "Of course not! I left you a note on your fridge. I....just thought that you didn't want to see me before I left."

His eyes flashed as he fisted his hand into her hair and shook his head. "If you believe that then you don't know me very well!" He pulled her into a passionate kiss that took her breath, she had never experienced a kiss that had touched her to that extent.

———m———

Drina sat on her stool, guitar in her lap, playing one of her newest songs. *'My Rider'*. The entire band, (Ben on guitar, Riley on the fiddle, Brón on the drums, and Grayson on the keyboard) played along with her. This one song had been inspired by Beau, and it was turning out to be the band's favorite. They all knew it would be a hit.

Together the women sang the chorus -

"There he goes my Rider to the gate....where he will meet his lady with the bull of fate.

To defeat this Titan who awaits within the chute, he bows his head and prays for the gift of strength from You.

Only one man can beat danger at it's own game.

My Bull Rider knows his one true fate.

When he calls, this Titan of death, my Rider will answer without fear of losing his breath.

A man of honor, a warrior with courage and faith.

Only one man can beat danger at it's own game.

My Rider knows his one true fate."

———m———

After the practice, the band joined Drina for lunch at her favorite café. "Drina," Gray smiled, "Are you sure this is what you really want to do? I mean....I've known you; your whole life, and all you've ever wanted to do was sing."

Riley nodded, "In high school you were always the winner of every talent show."

Ben chuckled, "I bet you were helping her though. Right? She had no competition. If you had sung against her....it would have been a close draw." His wife blushed.

Drina studied her friends and nodded with a grin. "Yes. I've learned something about myself over the last months. I enjoy song writing far more than I do the singing on stage. Riley has a better pitch and wider range of octives than I ever had. And, you're right, Ben. We were teamed up at all the talent shows. Only once did we not sing together, and that year....Riley won." They all laughted causing Riley's blush to deepen. "I'm tired of the touring. Don't get me wrong, I love you guys and I will always be willing to do a guest spot, or benefit concert, but I've just reached this point in my life where I need something different."

Brón nodded, "I have to admit that sometimes I need a break also. With all the weddin' plans and goin' on tour...." he looked down, "Ye feel like a worn out rubber band. Amy loves the life as much as I do.... but she wants to be married in Ireland. Not that I blame 'er....that is 'er homeland...."

Drina grinned, "Brón, why didn't you tell me you and Amy were engaged?" She hugged him and pulled out her cell to text the lady in question.

The drummer smiled, "Ye were at the ranch and I thought ye just needed a real break, ya know. Amy and I agreed that we would talk to ya when ye got back. We were hopin' that ye would sing at the weddin'." He cursed in his native tongue. "I'm not sayin' this very well."

Tears filled her eyes. She was beyond honored that they would ask her. "You said it beautifully. Well, when is the wedding and where?"

He beamed, "In two months time. April 4th. At her family's chapel in Dublin, Ireland....oh, I know....a Scotts Highlander marryin' an Irish Dancer, who can kick me ars. There must be somethin' wrong with me head."

Gray pulled out his keychain flashlight and shone it into the drummer's ear. In a fained exaggerated British accent he said, "Well, my dear Highlander.... according to my medical experience, there is nothing missing up here. If there were this innovative military grade flashomiter would have detected any problems, by shining through to the wall opposite your very large head."

The Scotsman smacked Grayson on the back of his head playfully. "Ye are very lucky that the lassies are watchin', lad."

The whole group began laughing. Drina sobered, "Let's see how things go here....if some things workout the way I hope...." Drina wasn't sure how this would work out. If she and Beau worked things out she would have to talk to him about this.

───∿∿∿───

Four days had passed since Drina had left and Beau was spending most of his days out on the range looking for wolf tracks with Hope or working out in his personal gym. Right now he lay on his weight bench pumping a hundred pounds as Rowdy spotted him. Normally he could bench press more than this, (when he was at his best) but right now he was still bouncing back from the pneumonia.

He counted under his breath and he pushed the bar back up, sweat running down his arms. When he knew he had reached his limit for the time being he nodded to his spotter and Rowdy helped him return the bar to its resting position. He sat up and accepted the bottle of water.

"Thanks."

Rowdy sat across from his boss and best friend. "Don't ya think you're goin' at this all the wrong way, bro." At a warning look from Beau he dove in head first before the other man could shut him up. "Look, you're not one hundred percent yet, and pushin' yourself like this will do more harm than good."

"I have to get back up to full strength. There's too much to do, too much at stake." He sighed and shook his head. "He's out there, Rowdy; plannin', waitin'. He's not done yet. He means to take us down. He has too much to lose. He knows the girls can testify and....I don't know for sure, but I don't think they were the first children he had molested. I think usin' the wolves to help with the rustling began here though."

Rowdy sighed, "I know. We need to really get our asses in gear and start trainin' again. Times like this I'm glad most of our men are retired and honorably discharged Special Forces."

Beau nodded, "Koni and the crew has made a lot of head way. She has put together a top notch team of deputes and they're puttin' the pieces of the puzzle together."

"Yes, but what has that got to do with you killin' yourself like this?" Rowdy asked.

Before Beau could answer Lillie wheeled herself into the gym. "Beau Sebastian Blanton! I've given you four days to wake up and do right by her!" Her face was red and she pointed her finger into her youngest son's bare chest. "I have had it up to here with your stubbornness!" She raised her hand over her head.

Beau and Rowdy were both shocked at the change in the older woman. Yancy on the other hand was grinning at the dumbfounded looks on the younger men's faces.

Lillie glared up at her son. She meant business. Beau recalled in all his years she only called him by his full name when he was in serious trouble, and from the look of things this time would forever rank in the top three.

"The Lord sent Drina to you, for a reason! You love her and you just let her up and leave, she was just waiting for you to stop her, and you never did! What does that tell her? Hmmmm!" Lillie poked his chest before he could even think of answering, "I tell you what....it means.... You don't care or you are a scaredy cat! That's what it means! Your father was stubborn too, but he had the guts to sweep me off my feet! You're kidding yourself, son; by hiding away in here! You love her and you know it! Now Cowboy Up, or Ranger Up! Which ever way you want to look at it! Just get your ass in gear and go after your perfect match, or you'll regret it the rest of your life!"

She glared at Rowdy. The young man's eyes were just as wide as Beau's and his jaw just as open. "You, young man have horses to see to! Now get!" She pointed to the door with one finger.

"Yes, ma'am!" Rowdy, Beau both said and stood making a mad dash for the exit.

<hr />

Once outside Yancy let his laughter show. "That was a damn nice smack down, honey."

Lillie grinned. "Brett's mama gave him one much the same way. I was in the next room and was about to leave when she told me to pay very good attention. Because; one day my own son would need the same talkin' to." Both broke into heart warming laughter.

———ᶜ∭ᵕ———

Beau burst from his mud room and into the kitchen, where the twins and Ava sat playing 'Horses in a Hat' Kyle was in the midst of a move as they all looked up at him, concern writen all over their faces.

"Kids, pack your thin's! Enough for a week or so. We're going to a Valentine's Day Concert!" All three whooped and headed for their rooms to start packing.

CHAPTER TWENTY-SIX

**** Kyle cast a concerned look at Ava's pale face and gently placed his hand on her arm. "Are you feeling better, Ava?"

"Some, but I think my stomach is still at home." She said striving to put on a brave face.

"It's ok, Ava. Flying does kind of take some getting used to. I left my stomach behind a lot at first too." Kaylee said.

The kids were sitting together with Ava between the twins while Beau, and Bobbi sat directly behind them for access, should assistance be required.

Beau realized he shouldn't have worried about Ava. The twins were so good with her. The three fit together just like he, Brett, Rowdy, and Brody (Rowdy's elder twin) had as youngsters. So much so that Yancy had dubbed them, 'The Four Musketeers'. They loved it and he thought it made the twins really feel as if they were part of the ranch - like they really belonged. And to him, they did, in fact if things worked out he wanted to adopt them as well. He felt like all three of them were his children already. He couldn't believe his life had changed so much....so wonderfully since that little songbird had stepped foot on the 3B ranch.

He smiled and looked at the engagement ring his mother had presented to him before they left.

"Have you thought about an engagement ring? You can't very well propose and not have one."

"I, I really haven't had time to think much about it mom there's been so many things to arrange. Why?"

Lillie had placed a small red velvet box in his hand. He flipped the lid up and look at the beautiful ring.

I don't know if you remember it sweetheart, but this is the ring your dad gave me when he proposed. He knew how much I treasured my Irish heritage and found this." She looked at the ring lovingly and smiled.

It featured three diamonds together to form a heart, flanked by a three pointed Celtic knot on either side. It was made of steel to better stand up to the riggers of ranch life.

"I've been saving it all these years. I knew the right time would come to bring it out and I think your father would love for Drina to wear it when she joins our family."

"Mom," Beau said choking up, I would love to put this on her hand, but don't you think Bobbi would want it?"

"No." Bobbi said walking into the room. "Mom asked me about it the other day when you announced you had wised up and was going after her. I love the idea of her wearing it and she'll appreciate it's history."

"You're sure, Bobbi? You have to be sure." He said wiping a tear before it fell onto his cheek.

"I am absolutely, one hundred percent sure. I love that she has made you so happy and she just...." she waved her hands searching for the right words, "fits, she fits you and the ranch. She belongs here with you. They all belong here with you....with us. And this...." she pointed to the ring. "would tie her to all of us from the beginning. I think daddy would approve." She said looking at their mother who nodded in agreement.

Beau nodded and was in the process of putting the box in his pocket when the kids trooped in and announced they were packed and ready to go.

"What's that?" Asked the ever curious Kyle. Beau thought a moment before holding it to them. "It's the engagement ring I hope to put on Drina's finger. Think she'll like it?"

"Yes!"

"Oooh, pretty!"

"Heck, yeah!" They all said at once grinning from ear to ear, growing more excited with every minute.

"Me too," he grinned. "So we're all ready?" He asked. "Ok then, let's giddy up and go!"

"Yes!" They agreed again together. They all said their good byes and piled into Beau's big truck after loading Ava's travel wheelchair.

———✠———

Beau flipped the box closed and returned it to his pocket. "You ok up there, Tadpole?" He asked, smiling at the way all three were talking and laughing together.

"I'm fine now, dad. I don't know why I was so nervous."

"The fear of the unknown." He said in his best theatrical voice, which brought another bought of laughter.

"Are we there yet?" Kyle asked the stewardess as she offered drinks and snacks.

———✠———

Ben met them at the airport. "I told Drina I had to pick up a gift for Riley, and could she keep her occupied for a while for me." He chuckled, "She was all too ready to help out." He looked at the kids and clapped his hands together, "Are we ready for this or what?" And laughed at their excited and the immediate response. He would be sorry to see Drina leave the band, but he knew how much happier she had been since meeting Beau and was glad that she had found someone to help shoulder the responsibility for the twins. The cowboy was good for her and would take care of his friend.

Beau came back with a luggage rack, airport assistant and Ava's wheelchair.

"I reserved a three part suite of rooms. Bobbi and girls can bunk in one, Kyle and Eli in one and you in the other. They're on the same floor as ours and are all connected, so supervision will be easy and convenient."

"Supervision?" Kyle asked aghast. "We don't need supervision! What'd ya think we are - babies?"

Always fast on his feet Ben answered smoothly, "It'll just make it easier to stay out of sight so the surprise won't be spoiled."

"Uh-huh." Kyle answered, not entirely mollified.

"Besides," Beau answered, "four eleven year olds on their own is a scarey thought." He fained a shiver of horor. "After all, this is a huge city and a huge hotel and I'm not takin' any chances of losing any of my kids. Besides," he added as Kyle and Kaylee straightened their shoulders and stood taller, "It'll make it easier for Ava to get around without havin' to go out in the hall."

They all knew a moment of utter panic when they were checking in. They were all headed to the elevator when Kyle, who was in the lead suddenly turned around and began pushing everyone back.

"Oh glory be! Drina's coming! Scram! Hide!"

Kaylee and Ava scurried into the nearby pool area and hid behind a screen, while Kyle squatted behind a large potted plant. Beau sat quickly and became engrossed in a newspaper.

Ben was breathless upon meeting Drina in the lobby.

"Oh!" She said startled.

"Drina!" He said smiling nervously. "Hi."

"Hi, yourself. I was getting worried about you, we need to be headed over to the arena in just a few minutes." She said looking at him. "Did you get Riley's surprise? What is it? I can't wait to see it."

"Surprise?" Ben asked blankly. "What surpri-i, oooh!" He laughed nervously and ran his hand through his hair as she looked at him.

"The surprise! Yeah! No, no I didn't. They got it all messed up and I had to reorder it!"

"Reorder it?" She asked looking at him oddly. "Ben, are you all right? You seem a little flushed. Do you feel ok?" She asked placing a hand on his forehead.

"Never better, never better, babe. Just upset that they screwed things up, that's all." He said, waving Kyle back when he noticed the boy peeking up through the large ferns. Drina noticed the direction he was looking and motioning so frantically and started to turn to look also.

Ben grabbed and turned her around and began rushing her back to the elevator, "Uh, we need to finish getting ready, Drina. Geez we're gonna' be late."

The crowd went wild stomping, clapping and yelling their approval of the last song. They were an hour and a half into the Valentine's Day concert with thirty minutes left and the crowd showed no sign of being ready for it to end.

The band changed the tempo and sang a tried and true favorite for many years, 'I love how you love me.' The fans quieted immediately and began to sway and sing along.

Drina loved it when the twins were able to be in the crowd. Tonight was bitter sweet because even though the twins, Ava, and, Bobbi were there, Beau was not. As the song ended, she called Riley to stand with her.

"I can't begin to tell you how much your welcome, love, and support means to me - to all of us in the band. Everyone here will be the first to know of some exciting new changes that we're making. I imagine most of you know that I have had guardianship of my eleven year old brother and sister for a while now, and I....I find that I need to give them a more stable environment to grow up in than being on tour ten months out of the year. Also I think most of you know that I write most of our songs and I am going to continue doing that as well as for some other people."

The crowd was beginning to mutter and whisper. "Aw come on Drina don't quit on us now." Came from a female voice somewhere in the audience which was taken up by two thirds of the audience.

She raised her hands for quiet. "Please, I'm not quitting, I'm just cutting back on touring and personal appearances and spending more of that time writing songs and doing home work and being with my kids."

Oh, the crowd was not happy to hear that and began muttering louder.

"Please, don't misunderstand, the band will continue as usual, it will be led by Riley here as lead singer. She's actually better than I am and I know you will continue to love and support us as you always have. For now, we'd like to perform for you a brand new song that I wrote recently. I hope you enjoy it as much as we do." And they began to sing, *'My Rider.'*

"In this Rodeo call life we are all the same riding our own Bulls of Fate. But one Rider always stands out.

He removes his hat before each ride and kneels before his Lord.

With hat to his heart, and voice lifted in song, he praises the One who rose high on a cross.

He then bravely goes to the gate....where he will meet with the bull of fate.

To defeat this Titan who awaits within the chute, he bows his head and prays for the gift of strength from You.

The Bull Rider knows his one true fate.

When he calls this Titan of death, The Rider will answer without fear of losing his breath.

A man of honor, a warrior with courage and faith.

He stands up tall facing down the danger, heart filled with the knowledge that Your love makes him stronger.

With each power filled step, The Rider comes closer to his possible death.

With eyes of fire the Titan watches each stride.

Heart filled with malice the Titan plans the Rider's last breath.

There he goes The Rider to the gate....where he will meet the Titan of fate.

To defeat this Bull who awaits within the chute, he bows his head and prays for the gift of strength from You.

The Rider knows his own true fate.

When he calls, this Titan of death, The Rider will answer without the fear of losing his breath.

A man of honor, a warrior with courage and faith.

Now to battle he goes the winner only You may know.

Now he drops to one knee, and gives thanks for his victory.

For he knows that without Your love this war would never have been won.

Now The Rider knows his one true fate.

As the song ended the audience was utterly silent until....the crowd erupted in screaming, stomping and clapping as flowers and small stuffed toys landed on the stage. The ovation went on for five minutes as Drina wiped tears of happiness for the total acceptance of her song and sadness for missing Beau.

Something caught Ben's attention back stage, he and the band smiled and Ben gave a half salute before joining Drina, and Riley.

"We're sure glad you like that song as much as we do. We have another surprise now." While Ben smiled and talked to the crowd, Drina's mind was racing. Surprise? What other surprise? She knew of no other surprise. What was going on here? Being out of the loop was grating on her nerves.

Ben turned his guitar upside down on his back as he took center stage. "How many rodeo fans do we have here tonight?" Two thirds of the audience yelled, whistled and clapped.

"All right!" A huge grin spead across his face, "How many of you are Bull Riding fans?" Once again the crowd erupted into clapping, stomping, whistling, and yelling.

"That's what I thought," Ben said smiling even wider. "How many of you watched the PBR's Championship rodeo last year?" (Cheering, clapping, and whistling).

Ben laughed, "Yeah, it was pretty awesome, huh?" (Cheering, clapping, stomping, and whistling).

"Yeah! All right! Do you remember who won the Championship buckle? Who beat Good Ol' Boy at his own game."

There was a resounding, "Beau Blanton!" and couple people in the crowd yelled, "Let's giddy up and go!" And once again there was cheering, stomping, and whistling.

"Yeah! That's what I'm talking about." Ben yelled. "Well, we have a special surprise for Drina tonight."

Drina gasped and stared at Ben. "What is going on? Ben, what did you do?!"

"Did you know that Beau can sing?" Ben asked, looking out at the crowd. She was still trying to figure out what was happening. He smiled, "Man, can he sing...." he looked at the crowd, "Do you want to see the current Bull Riding Champ and be the first to hear him sing?!" Drina's jaw dropped as if it finally hit her.

The crowd went wild. It wasn't long before they were all chanting, "Beau, Beau, Beau, Beau!"

Ben looked out to grin at the crowd then leaned into his mic and yelled out, "It is my great pleasure, and honor to introduce to you....my friend....Mr. Beau Blan-tooon!"

He pointed to the right with a flourish, and the crowd went wild as Beau calmly walked out on stage a guitar slung across his back, and shook Ben's hand.

He lifted a mic to his lips and yelled to the crowd as he raised a hand high. "Hello, Nashviiiille!" The crowd cheered. "What an honor it is, to be here tonight with Drina at the Grand Ol' Opry. Home of Country Music!" The crowd roared.

He smiled and waved to the crowd before turning to Drina, she was dumbstruck and could not help the tears. The singer ran a few steps and threw her arms around his neck, he in turn wrapped his arms around her, picked her up and spun her around. The crowd, already giving Beau a standing ovation, suddenly erupted into screaming and shouting. Ben had to step forward and raise his hands for silence.

"Give her a kiss, Beau." Came from somewhere in the crowd.

"Yeah, giddy up an go, Beau!" Came from another audience member.

"Kiss, kiss, kiss, kiss!" Filled the air.

Taking the opportunity and loving the feel of holding her in his arms Beau kissed her with all the love he had to give in one, gentle, sweet, wonderful kiss that took her breath away and touched her down to her toes.

Wolf whistles filled the air as the crowd cheered for their happy reunion.

When Beau and Drina separated, they stepped apart, fingers still entwined. The crowd, knowing something momentous was about to happen became quiet and watchful.

The cowboy spoke into his mic. His eyes never leaving her's. "I've thought a lot about how it felt to say goodbye to you last week." He looked her steadily in the eyes and ran his fingers gently down her cheek, catching the tears. "I've decided I can't do that anymore, I don't want to say goodbye to you ever again. So....I have something to tell you and something to ask you after this...."

And with that, Ben brought a stool out and Beau took his seat in front of the mic. He strummed his guitar and began to play George Strait's, 'When Love Cross' My Heart', after a few cords he began to sing in his clear baritone. The crowd was enchanted, by his voice and by the love that floated in the air.

When it was time for the chorus the entire band quietly joined him with their instruments. Grayson added the piano, Ben, his guitar, Brón the drums, and Riley added the fiddle. The sound was unlike anything Drina had ever heard in her life. Ben, Grayson, and Brón pulled their mics close, and began to sing the chorus along with Beau. The four voices blended like they were meant to be a team. Four voices in perfect harmony.

The crowd stood once again, and began to sway to the beat. Women holding the hands of their husbands, and boyfriends. Teenage girls wiping tears away. Some even sang along softly with Beau.

Drina wiped tears away as the chorus started once again. Their voices blending like they were made to work together. She would be shocked if Beau wasn't begged to start singing professionally after tonight.

Back home Rowdy, Yancy, Lillie, and the rest of the 3B watched on TV as their boss sang into the microphone. Pouring his heart and soul into the song.

When he played the final notes the crowd erupted in a way they never had before. Their voices rising to meet the heavens, yelling Beau's name over and over again.

Drina still had tears tracking down her face. She had always loved this song and he knew it, from here on out, this was their song. It would forever be symbolic of their willingness to spend the rest of their lives together.

'Oh, how I love this man.' She thought.

After the song was over, Beau stood, handed his guitar to Riley, gracefully dropped to one knee and pulled the little red, velvet jewelers box from his jeans pocket.

"I talked to the kids," he said softly while the audience paid rapt attention. "I told the kids how much I loved you...and them. I asked Ava, Kaylee and Kyle's permission to marry you."

She took a shaky breath, "And what did they say?"

From the front row the twins and Ava yelled together, "Yes! Yes! Yes!"

The audience laughed and tears were wetting cheeks all over the auditorium.

Bobbi grinned so happy for her brother and wishing both her father and oldest brother could be there to see this.

"What do ya say, sweetheart? Will you come to the ranch, become part of it...part of me? Will you marry me?"

Tears streaming down her cheeks, she laughed, nodded and whispered, "Yes!"

The crowd jumped to their feet as one and began clapping, whistling, cheering and laughing. Beau slipped the ring on her finger, stood and took her in his arms and kissed her. They held each other tightly and Beau looked up toward the heavens and mouthed, "Thank You, Lord."

He had finally found his way, and now knew he had God to thank for it. Drina had ended his lonliness, she had given him three children to love as his own and brought him back to the Lord. How could any man be more blessed?

CHAPTER TWENTY-SEVEN

Six months later -

**** Drina stood in her cabin with Riley, Amy, Bobbi, Ava, and Kaylee. All of whom looked in the mirror at the Western Wedding attire the bride wore, an ivory colored suede skirt and matching vest. The blouse was off white with matching antique lace that fell from the shoulders and formed a V on front and back. She turned and tugged on the skirt and watched it flare out around her. It fell just below the knees with the self fringe.

She had found off white boots with the same fringe on the top and were a perfect match for her dress. Her outfit was topped by an ivory colored lace hat with bridal veil secured by a lace butterfly. She had seen a picture of it on the internet while looking at bridal dresses with the girls and had loved it. There were a few changes she wanted and while talking with Bobbi one day she had discovered that Amanda, (one of the hand's wives), worked as a seamstress.

She had been thrilled to be asked to make the bridal clothes, and as the couple also lived on the ranch, fittings were convenient. Drina posed for pictures as the outfit was being made and then, in the finished product, hoping to help the young woman further her craft and put a jumpstart on her own business. The pictures were put on display in the store and on her website. Soon, so many requests for Amanda's sewing skills began coming in that the store helped her open her own shop with a provision that she provide alterations for the store's customers. A business of her own was a dream that Amanda thought would never come true. The fact made Drina's wedding day even more meaningful.

"Are you sure this buckskin skirt is right? I mean, is it too western?" Drina asked for the hundredth time.

Her friends laughed, "Honey, Beau's not going to be looking at the skirt." Riley said.

Bobbi nodded. "He is just as nervous as you are, sweety. Rowdy said Beau keeps asking him to make sure you haven't gotten cold feet and flown the coop."

Amy (Brón's new wife) smiled and rubbed her small baby bump, "Aye lass. But I thought that was what ye planned. The Western look I mean."

The other women chuckled, even Ava and Kaylee joined in the fun. "You look beautiful." The new sister's chorused.

Only a few days before Drina, Beau and the kids had appeared before Judge Taylor. After talking to them and all three eleven year olds, he ordered that the adoptions be finalized. They had gone out to dinner afterwards and celebrated as an official family. Ava, Kaylee, and Kyle were all Blantons.

The bride grinned. "I keep thinking that I'm going to wake up, and it will just all be a dream."

"Oh, this is no dream, dear." Lillie said as she wheeled herself into the room. "I have a gift for the bride."

Beau tossed the chaps back at Rowdy for what seemed like the twentieth time. "I'm not wearin' those chaps. Drina would kill me, then I'd kill you!"

"Just tryin' to help ya out, boss." Rowdy said smirking. The nervous groom paced back and forth in his cabin.

Yancy and Rowdy tried hard not to laugh. "Son, if ya don't feel right, just don't wear 'em. The Tux, and the black Stetson....well, that's just fine. But, you'll never hear the end of it if you forget to wear your Pop's bolo tie."

Kyle held up the tie and beamed at his new father. "Can I help?"

Beau knelt down and allowed his son to put the bolo tie with the turquoise stone around his neck. Lillie had found the stone before she and Brett Sr. had married, and had it made into the bolo tie for their wedding. Beau then helped him tighten it and grinned as they looked into the mirror together.

"Well, son. How do I look?"

Kyle beamed, "Like a cowboy in trouble...." All the men in the room laughed. Kyle looked shyly up at his hero. "But, for a dad....you look.... awesome!"

Beau grinned and helped the boy with his own tie, and jacket. As a surprise Beau had purchased matching black Western Tuxedos, boots, and stetsons, for himself and Kyle. The boy hadn't stopped grinning yet.

There was a soft knock on the door. Beau called, "Enter," leftover habit from his days as a Ranger.

Ben walked in with Ava in his arms and a huge grin on his face. "Little Miss Ava wanted to come and see how our groom is doing, so we decided to come together." His grin widened and an evil gleam lit his eyes. "Ten minutes of freedom left! If you're gonna hop on that horse and sink spur, you better get movin'!"

Ava studied her father as if she had never seen him before. She placed her hand over her heart, her big blue eyes met his, and she said breathlessly. "Oh, daddy....you look....hot!"

A look of shock crossed over his face, and heat climbed up his neck, as wolf whistles and cat calls filled the cabin. "Hot?...Well....uh...."

Kyle whispered into his ear, "That means you look real good." He said trying to ease his father's mind.

The groom grinned and whispered to Kyle, "You got the rings, son?"

Kyle smiled and patted his pocket "Yup! Right here."

"Good man!" The new father said and they gave each other a high five. Then Beau turned back to Ava, "Thanks, honey....I think. And you look lovely." He turned back to Kyle after glaring at the Bestman and Groomsmen. "Don't you think your sister looks pretty, Kyle?"

The boy shugged, "Ehhhh, I guess she looks ok....for a girl."

Ben chuckled and sat the little girl on her father's piano, as both Rowdy and Nate began wiping invisible lint from their boss's jacket.

"Oooo yeah, hot indeed!" Rowdy said winking at Ava, who giggled.

Nate licked his finger, touched the end to Beau's shoulder and said, "Ssssssssssss."

'I need a shovel.' The groom thought.

Bear Black Feather reached around from behind Beau, pinched and shook his cheek. "He's just such a cute wittle groom!" He said.

They all laughed at the scowl the groom shot the Deputy. Beau moved like lightning, one minute Bear was laughing at the older cowboy, and the next....Beau took him down with a hip throw.

The kid landed hard on his back at Kyle's feet with an, "Ooooff!"

At the show of strength Kyle's face lit up. "Coooool! Nice moves, dad!" He called out giving Beau two thumbs up.

"Laugh it up, Bear!" Beau snapped at the downed Groomsmen. "What will you tell your sister when I have Yancy call her in here?!" He glared at his men, "Or maybe I could leave and have Bobbi and Drina come deal with all you boys?!" He nodded when the laugher instantly died down, until he turned away.

Ava crossed her arms and gave a long suffering sigh, "Dad, seriously!"

The younger man laying at the groom's feet started laughing once more at the child's serious tone. "Yeah, dad! Seriously." He winked at the little lady.

Ava having had a long time crush on the big man blushed and gave him a small smile.

Her father turned to her and shugged, saying innocently, "He started it."

Rowdy slapped him on the shoulder. "We got your back, bro."

Beau grinned, and bent to help Bear to his feet, slapping the larger man on the back hard, and calling out to all his teammates and friends, "Rangers!"

All the rangers past, present, (and future) answered in unison. "Lead the way!"

Beau stood waiting in the gazebo with the minister and Rowdy standing by his side. Yancy, Bear, and Nate were his Groomsmen. Between Rowdy and Yancy was a space that would be filled by Kyle once the boy escorted his sisters down the aisle.

Beau smiled to himself when he felt his father's energy in the air. How he wished his pop, Brett, Brody could be here with him today.

'Well, dad.' He looked up the hill at the apple tree where his father, and Rowdy's brother rested. *'I'm gettin' married today. We wanted to have the ceremony here so you can be with us. You said one day I would understand what it means to need more than just the ranch.'* He smiled, *'Now I do. Thanks....for helpin' Drina when you did. You'll always be welcome in our home, and we're counting on you to help with these kids, and those still to come.'*

As if in answer Beau felt a stong hand squeeze his left shoulder. Stunned he turned, but no one was touching him. With a start he knew who that squeeze had been from. 'Thanks, dad.'

After the bridesmaids and Bobbi were positioned in the gazebo, the band began to play the Wedding March. Beau was amazed again at how beautiful his lady was. He couldn't believe she would be his in a few moments. Ben led her down the aisle, a huge grin on his face.

Drina was less nervous playing in front of several thousand people. She took several deep breaths and tried to calm the shakes - until she saw Beau. The love in his eyes soothed her nerves like nothing else ever had.

As Drina reached the flower decked gazebo she placed a white rose in an empty chair in honor of her mother.

Just as the minister was winding up the ceremony, a soft breeze filled with the scent of apples blossems and swirled around the happy couple.

Drina closed her eyes and breathed it in. Brett Sr. was here with them, giving them his blessings, and there was another as well. A younger presence.

She heard a young voice in her ear, "Help Rowdy, help him understand. It was never his fault." Just then she felt as if someone had kissed her cheek.

Beau felt the soft, fragrant breeze surround them with love. He wondered if he could possibly be happier until he felt a hand squeeze his shoulder and gently pat his back. 'Brody.'

"And now, with the authority invested in me by our Almighty God and the State of Montana, it is my honor and privilege to pronounce you husband and wife." He smiled at Beau and was about to give permission to kiss his bride when Beau beat him to the punch.

He framed his wife's lovely little face with his hands and gently, lovingly kissed her forehead, her cheeks and finally looked deeply into her eyes. "I love you, Mrs. Blanton," and kissed her with all the love and tenderness he had to give.

The couple turned and stood while the minister said, "Ladies and gentlemen, boys and girls, "he turned and looked up at the hill, "and honored guests. I'd like to introduce for the first time Mr. and Mrs. Beau and Drina Blanton.

They smiled at each other and each of their children. As they stepped out of the gazebo, Drina gave a white rose to her new mother-in-law and they took their first walk together back down the aisle and waited for the wedding party to join them in celebrating the beginning of their new life together. Happily ever after.

EPILOGUE

**** High on the hill top, a man lay below the branches of the large Apple tree on the highest edge of the knoll. He wore a ghilly suit, and held military grade binoculars to his eyes. Beside him, rested a military sniper rifle. His black eyes watched as he took down notes for the boss.

He turned to level an evil glare at the stone that stood only feet from where he lay, he shoved his middle finger in the air at the stone while he smirked and fantasized showing the disrespect to the man resting at peace beneath the stone.

"You may have stopped us once, Blanton, but you sure can't stop us now. My father and I will have your ranch." He spat tobacco juice at the base of Brett Sr's head stone.

Little did he realize that two unseen Rangers leaned their shoulders against the tree, with arms crossed, they watched the sniper. Deputy Sam Dogg turned back to the festivities and began taking more notes.

'That idiot cowboy thinks he can just up and marry a rich little singing star! Where does she get off marryin' a millionaire rancher and foist her kid brother and sister off as his? Thinks he has the right to be happy? What gives her the idea that she can take what is rightfully mine!' He spit once more, 'They have no idea who they're dealin' with. You go ahead hayseed and enjoy it while you can.'

He reached for his rifle, aimed and was ready to take his shot.... when a soft breeze wafted past his face. The sweet breeze smelled of apple blossoms....but the tree had no blossoms....he looked around him. The deep disembodied voice of a young man, drifted in the wind and swirled around him.

"I wouldn't do that if I was you! Leave now, while you can. We'll give ya this one chance....use it well....Dogg!"

⸺✳⸺

Hope rose to her feet, hair stood up along her spine as she smelled the air sweeping down from Apple Hill. She growled deep and low and began stepping toward the hill.

Beau looked at Hope and then at the hill. Sheriff Koni, Bear and Hos also stood and smelled the air. They looked at each other and exchanged hand signals. "What is it girl?" He asked placing his hand on Hope's neck. Bear suggested that he let her go, check it out before the wedding guests and Drina noticed.

⸺✳⸺

Deputy Dogg turned white, scrambled up, and took off for his horse, leaving his notes scattered over the grave. At the last moment he reached down toward his rifle. His hand stopped midway when a large canine paw stepped on the barrel. He froze. With all the wolves they had raised and trained, he stared into the deadly eyes of the biggest wolf he had ever seen. When she growled and snarled....he had never seen bigger teeth or been more scared in his life.

The apple scented breeze swirled around the knoll and a different voice, an older voice echoed in his ears, *"Easy girl. Dogg, this is your chance. Go while you can."*

Dogg decided it would be better to live another day and bolted toward his horse, to the sound of laughter belonging to not just one man, but two. He decided not to tell his old man about how this stakeout ended. The boss would be mad, but they would always have other opportunities to take Blanton out.

After he mounted Dogg turned to look back at the hill. What he saw staring down at him terrified him far more than the wolf ever could.

⸺✳⸺

The two ghostly Rangers watched from the hill top. One was dressed in Bull Riding attire. Jeans, boots, spurs, vest, and cowboy hat. The younger of the two was in full battle gear. Helmet, vest, weapons (including his firearm), boots, and pack. He was still covered in the soot, smoke, dirt, and his own lifes blood, (which was optional depending on who he showed himself too). Reminders of the battle that took his life.

A battle that if ever given the chance, he would gladly fight again. Even now after death, he still viewed it as a great honor to have fought and died for his country, and his brother.

First Lieutenant Kincaid looked at the Major, and spoke his lips never once moving. *"He'll be back. His father is not one to give up so easily."*

Major Blanton nodded, *"Yes, Beau's lady knows where the files are now. It will be a few years before Rodriguez can make his final move, and by then they will have help....and not just from us."*

Kincaid nodded, *"Rowdy, is loosin' faith in himself. I'm afraid his resolve is weakening. I fear for my brother's sanity. My sister's as well. They are still not speaking. Trish is stubborn in her own way."*

Brett looked at the younger Ranger beside him. *"We serve the Big Man now. Trust that He knows what's to be done. We do as commanded. Don't worry, son....Rowdy will be fine. So will Patricia."*

With that they returned to their silent vigil.

⚬⚬⚬

Beau, Sheriff Koni and the Rangers, past and present, crept silently up the knoll. They covered the area looking for tracks and evidence when Beau discovered the rifle. Several began picking up the note paper, being careful to avoid adding their own fingerprints. Sheriff Koni picked up the rifle with gloved hands.

"We'll get all this to the lab and see if it yields anything for use." She turned to Beau, "Go on back to the reception and enjoy it. I'd be willing to bet this is tied in to the rustling. But worse....now we know someone has been marked for execution."

DEAR READERS

<hr/>

**** We thank you for reading, 'Cowboy Mine' and hope you enjoyed it as much as we loved the making of it.

This book is dedicated to the brave men and women of our military, past, present and future to whom we owe our freedom. Thank you all for your service and sacrifice.

We would like to thank Zack Conner, PBR Bull Rider who was kind enough to share his knowledge and expertise.

We would also like to thank America's Army Rangers (and all the other branches of our brave militay) for their brave, unquestioning loyalty, service and sacrifice to our country.

In loving memory of Gunnery Sgt. Garland Dean McKinney, US Marines retired. Brother-in-law and Uncle who was respected, admired and loved.

He survived the Vietnam War and Desert Storm and came home to us. It was the cancer that took him down.

"You are forever loved, and missed, Uncle Dean. Thank you for always being there and for your brave service. May you forever Rest in Peace. Also in memory of Warren Thomas Blanton Sr. Father-in-law, and grandfather. A man who gave the ultimate sacrifice, so we could be free. We regret having never met you. Thank you for your service."

Rebecca (Becca)

Linda (Lynn)

Mother and daughter (Best friends for life.)

Printed in the United States
By Bookmasters